IN THE SEASON OF BLOOD & GOLD

IN THE SEASON OF BLOOD & GOLD

Stories

TAYLOR BROWN

Press 53
Winston-Salem

Press 53, LLC
PO Box 30314
Winston-Salem, NC 27130

First Edition

Copyright © 2014 by Taylor Brown

All rights reserved, including the right of reproduction in whole or in part in any form except in the case of brief quotations embodied in critical articles or reviews. For permission, contact author at Editor@Press53.com, or at the address above.

Cover design by Steffen Kuronen

Cover art, "It's a Fence Monday (Explored)," Copyright © 2011 by Jorunn Sjofn, used by permission of the artist.

Author photo by Ben Galland

This is a work of fiction. Names, characters, places, and incidents are products of the author's imagination or are used fictionally. Any resemblance to actual events, locales, or persons, living or dead, is entirely coincidental.

Printed on acid-free paper
ISBN 978-1-941209-04-2

for Mom and Dad

ACKNOWLEDGMENTS

Grateful thanks to the editors of the publications listed below for first publishing the following stories:

"Black Swan" first appeared in *The Dead Mule School of Southern Literature*.

"Home Guard" first appeared in *The Liars' League*.

"Rider" first appeared in *CutBank* and received the 2009 Montana Prize in Fiction.

"Whorehouse Piano" first appeared in *Pindeldyboz*.

"Kingdom Come" first appeared in the *2010 Press 53 Open Award Anthology* and received Second Prize in the 2010 Press 53 Open Awards for Short Story.

"River of Fire" first appeared in *storySouth*.

"Covered Bridge" first appeared in *Porchlight*.

"Bone Valley" first appeared in *The Bacon Review*.

"The Vizsla" first appeared in *The New Guard* and was a finalist for the 2012 Machigonne Fiction Prize.

"The Tattooist's Daughter" first appeared in *The Coachella Review*.

IN THE SEASON OF BLOOD & GOLD

RIDER	1
KINGDOM COME	11
THE TATTOOIST'S DAUGHTER	21
BONE VALLEY	33
THE VIZSLA	45
BLACK SWAN	55
SIN-EATERS	61
RIVER OF FIRE	77
WHOREHOUSE PIANO	97
HOME GUARD	103
COVERED BRIDGE	111
IN THE SEASON OF BLOOD & GOLD	125

RIDER

Iron-shod hooves stove the old wagon road, rock-jeweled, like gunshots. That sound lying in ambuscade in her chest for so long arrived now out of a quadrant near alien to the meat where she stored him. Her heart.

She slunk out of bed with the quilt left behind and then the gown shed too so that when he knocked and entered soundless with the night all over him in a cold aura she was warm where she touched him. She did her best to brush the night from his vestments, his skin, and flush the blood into the white of him, his coldest places, and the red fluid came like the blush of something killed in all that snow out of which he rode.

Blooded she knew him. Not him but what he was. A man. Another.

"I know you," she whispered to him. A rider. But he did not hear her.

He was a being borne of night alone and by the very first delineation of black timber to timber he rose furtive from slumber and stood stark white in the little cabin, a thing untouched by light but luminous itself. Always she was watching the black pines beyond the window and wanting to slow the turning of night to day. But the wanting seemed only to quicken the first stalks of light where they grew upward between the black trunks of pine.

In his emptied bedspace only the shotgun, old double Damascus that divided them, too cold to warm. This instrument of spurious fidelity that let them take rest in the wake of their coupling. This hated thing, she twined her heated limbs around the black steel and stock and the empty chambers moaned when she blew across the barrels.

The geese were snow geese, white as the driven when he shot them from the sky. He did so in dead of night. Ambush. His was a poacher's blind hidden from man and bird both. Not his wife though. She knew what scarce meat he preyed upon in fields not his own, and forbidden. Or thought she did.

His horse was a fine one, black and masculate. A cut above his station. Into the outlands he rode it, the terrain black and silver, mud and pond. There he spotted the earth with the night's kill, birds fresh fallen and white where punctures red-welled into feather and barb. On the return, he stopped at the lone cabin yellow-lit like a single soul in all those wilds. This his long custom.

A December night he quilted the horse against the cold, flesh-cutting as it was, and lay down in the bed not his own. Hers. In the morning the horse was dead standing stiff-legged and frozen and the geese, unsacked, were conjoined in severe attitudes of flight and death, moiled, a single frozen ménage of rendering so morbid and perverse it might sicken the hardest of heart, yet sculpted of brute and natural force.

"Would you look at that?" she said. "I've a mind to pray over them."

"Wouldn't none of it happened you'd of let me stow them in the house," he said.

The first night together she'd told him she'd not have his kill inside.

"That was a long time ago I said that," she said.

He spat. "Still holds, though. Don't it."

It was not a question.

She watched him drag his ice-laden kill down the road, the frozen jumble of wing and beak and claw straining the sack at mean angles, unforgiving shapes, and scrawling black vents of earth in the snowed-over road. Later the first shoots of daylight punctured the dawn-dark trees and struck the rigored horse on the big flanks, the serrated mane, the ice-glazed eyes of black marble devoid of all life. She tracked the dead thing thaw by its lips, black ones agape in death, pincering them between thumb and forefinger at intervals. In minutes they'd gone gummy again, like storebought licorice. Soon thereafter the first leg gave way, buckling, and the others, still rigid, crackled like trees overwrought with storm-ice. She leapt from harm as the black horse hove toward the buckling leg, a front one, and crashed headlong into the snow aside her cabin, lying there bloodless and alien as something hewn from black rock. Too heavy to move; she shoveled snow to hide it from passers on the road, should there be any.

He trudged onward through the snow, cursing the woman, the horse, the sudden freeze, the very sky that fed him. The food upon his back, the food tugged willy-nilly through the snow. He cursed them all. Rivulets of melted snow slid over the rim of his boot shafts, sliding down to pool in his soles, cold beyond all imagining. All was white but for the black stalks shot upright out of the snow in their groves, their huddled stands, the naked reaches of them groping skyward. The ashen sky. Geese hooted southward in their droves. He cursed them.

The road wound rightward ahead. Then the covered

bridge he crossed always at night, the divider of this outland, private-owned, from those safe for a man of his burden. Here he existed in sin. Hunting, riding, trudging, coupling. All trespass. All sin. There, the far side of the river, lay absolution. The law of man required proof, after all. Who was to say which side of the river the geese were flying when he killed them?

The bridge was very pretty with the new snow so heavy on its roof. Through the slatted wood beneath his boots he saw the black hiss of the river white-whorled with snowmelt. His bounty of fowl slid easily on the hardwood, unimpeded by root or ice. The bodies had begun to thaw, go deferential to his aims, fewer edges to snag. He cursed them still for their weight.

The shadowed tunnel, at least, gave comfort to a man of his nocturnal workings. Never had he dared to cross in daylight. Rich men paid astronomical sums to hunt the richness of the land he poached, and men richer still paid to protect the wealth of blood and fur and feather that abounded there. What he lacked in fortune he made up in daring, cunning, quick aim. He would return home, he thought, and distribute the snow geese among his kin like Old Saint Nick of fable. Christmas Eve, after all.

A good distance on the other side of the river he heard the staccato racket of horses on the bridge behind him. Hoof shots rang out of the covered maw like sudden ambush. He did not curse. No. He showed the whites of his teeth a moment to himself and hid them. Then he turned to see, as any man would. They rode three abreast, dark silhouettes under the bridge. The sun, stowed away beyond a pallid veil of cold, threw light enough to illumine them white-faced and black-coated when they rode from under the raftered dark. He glanced only a moment and turned away. As any man would.

The chestnut machines they rode slowed to a trot around him, the hot-breathed exhaust of their lungs audible to a man staring only at the road ahead. One, the leader, rode ahead and turned his big horse broadside the walker.

"Ho," said the warden. "What have you in the bag, sir?"

He stopped but did not open the bag.

"And a Merry Christmas to you gentlemen," he said.

The one in front of him tugged his jacket to reveal the white half moon of a revolver handle, ivory-gripped, protruding butt-first from his belt holster.

"What have you in the bag, sir?"

"Christmas gifts."

"Of what species?"

"Goose."

"Dump them out."

"Now this is public land. Your jurisdiction ends at the river—"

The warden drew the pistol from his belt and cocked the hammer and aimed the bottomless well of the barrel at the man's chest.

"Dump them out."

As told, he turned to dump the contents of the sack. There on the road behind him lay tell-tale rivulets of thaw blood, red on the white road, maddeningly red, a bright ribbon tethering him to the wrong side of the river as surely as a noose of rope or chain.

"Sin finds you out," said the warden.

He looked up at the men so tall on their horses. His shotgun was broken-barreled over his shoulder, unloaded. No other means of quick escape at hand. He dumped out his booty, birds of tundra red-painted in their own death. The fluid once binding them poured out alongside, a pink-watered blush in the snow. There was nothing more sculpted here, bodies gone slack.

"Please don't put me away," he told them. "I'll do anything."

The leader decocked his pistol and holstered it.

"Anything?" he said.

When she lay down that night she could not take her rest. The wild geese clutched so meanly in death, like birds huddled close against the cold. A wing here or there wavered slowly out of this image of them, feathers ice-serrated into a blade, and the honks of their kind choked from their beaks in strange bergs of goose speak. She wished she could warm them over the flames, restore tenderness and even flight, for the old tales told of beings long preserved in blocks of ice. Prehistoric things resurrected from centuries of cold fixation, minds frozen on one solid thought.

The geese were her friends. Always had been. But she could never touch them, altitude too high. Now she slept with one of their hunters. Nay, a poacher. She loved him. Wished to mend him from the bloodless chill within him and without. Make him supple and pinkened. No stranger to the sunlight of her backdoor. No stranger to the sun at all. Like her. A worshipper of sun and animal, of animate earth. Upon her roof stood a rough-hammered weathervane of a mythic bird, a phoenix, invisible at night.

She rose from bed and slid her feet into the boots of her husband, a decade dead, and cloaked herself in every article of clothing at hand. The night was milder, no harsh freeze, though all marks of travel along the road had been covered in a luminous down of snowfall. She crossed the covered bridge she'd crossed rarely since her husband, a warden, had been blown headless by a short 10-gauge at the mouth of this bridge. When she saw the peppered divots along the jambs and siding she halted and touched them. Bits of him might yet be buried in the minute scoriations of pine.

The road crested a white hill bristling with naked pine and then dropped into a valley. There in the white bowl of snowy hills lay the town. His town. The hilltops shone white under the moon and blued downward into a navy bottom against which the lights of town glimmered like a hand-scattering of gold bits. She started down, a slight woman mummified in thick tatterings of cloth.

She found his house easily. She asked some carolers. Said she had a gift to deliver from the outlands. As she walked in the direction pointed, the carols came angel-voiced over the rough-shod porches and snow, through the midnight-colored well of stars above them. Caroling faces black-gaped with song.

From the moon-shadowed lee of a neighboring house she watched him through the square yellow-lit glass of a back room. Crockery sat all around him. One by one, he removed the reddened geese from his sack and set them upon a cutting board. He cut off the wings and head and one foot, leaving the other as a handle. Then he plucked the feathers from the flanks, the back, the tail. In a pot over the fire he melted paraffin in boiling water, let cool, and dipped each goose into the viscous liquid. The remaining feathers dried laminate with wax and she watched him peel off that and the feathers, the down like peeling an orange. He cut a wide cavity from the rear vent and dug away the innards, saving hearts and livers in certain pots, various cuts of meat in others.

She watched him work long into the night, bent over his work. Goose breasts the size of a human heart smeared his hands red, the boon of Christmas morning. He handled the birds with great care, nothing vicious even in the plucking. The birds he flayed were slack-winged and jolly-necked, the meat red, those soft engines of flight coming free in shapes their own. His face reflected all of this, a colored complexion she'd not seen, whether of his own blood or that he worked she could not say.

She reached home by first light, carried there by thought of warmth in times past, warmth to come, warmth by virtue of more than fire alone.

At the door she looked where the big horse lay buried underneath the snow. Some might bury the thing but she knew the hollow pangs of winter and how many bellies on how many nights such a lot of meat could fill. She would leave it there in case. Not tell anyone. Not even him.

That day, in daylight, he came to her. Gift-bearing, she presumed, and welcomed him at the door. He was on another horse, a chestnut horse, and his face was ghost-white against the black of his scarf and hat.

"Let me warm you," she said, drawing him inside.

"Listen," he said. "Where is my horse?"

"Why?"

"Where is my horse?"

"Buried," she said.

"I need something to kill."

"What?"

"I need something to kill," he said. "I need the blood."

She grabbed his arm. "Listen to me," she said. "Are you crazy?"

"They think you are," he said. "That you're a witch. Scaring off the game. That's what they think. The wardens, the members."

"You're the one taking the game. You."

"You must leave," he said. "For good. Forever. I'll spread the blood in here and tell them I sank you in the river."

"I have rights to this land," she said. "By virtue of my husband."

He looked up the road and down. No one. He would

have to. He went back out to the horse and took the puppy from the sack, newborn, pink slits for eyes. When he went back inside she had the shotgun from the bed leveled on him.

"In the river," she said. "That's where they found him. What was left at least."

"Who?"

"My husband."

"I don't know nothing about it," he said. "They said to sink you—"

"I should of known," she said. "Goddamn you I should of known."

She primed both hammers with a heavy click and threaded her finger across the triggers, both of them.

His 12-gauge, as always, lay broken over his shoulder. Since the incident at the bridge he'd taken to keeping both barrels loaded. A precaution. And he knew what way to open her heart. All at once he tossed the puppy at her and let the shotgun slide off his shoulder into the crook of his arm. She extended an arm sideways to catch the splay-footed animal and opened her white breast to him and he jerked both barrels home with a heavy click, aiming for the heart.

The white wedge of the blast slammed into her chest, sledge-heavy, and tiny jets of matter, white-hot, sang quivering into the meat of her, her heart, her lungs, spreading like a white flock hatched in the blood. She wanted so badly to follow them south. Toward warmer skies, sunlight. The shotgun clattered to the floor. The puppy the bed. She looked a last time into his eyes and knew they were closer now than ever they'd been, than ever they'd be, and she turned from him, his red face, and staggered toward her back door, outward, into the light. The hard palate of earth was cold and black beneath the snow. Cold and black on her knees, her palms, her face. Then she was nothing but another sliver of it, earth-blackened and going cold.

In the spring of that year the snows melted late, later than ever, and riders passing along an outland trail, wardens, found a dark hulk of horse rising black-haunched from the diminishing snow alongside a small cabin. It rose from the snow complete, preserved by the cold, like something resurrected full-bodied from the grave. There were not many horses of such quality in short radius of this discovery; the owner was certain. The mane of the horse rose jagged and black, black as the blood found smeared inside the cabin.

KINGDOM COME

The boy dropped the knife into the stone mouth of the well and watched the blade glitter into the depths, blood from its edge red-clouding its wake, haunting the blade like tidings of its history. In seconds the implement disappeared into profound and lightless depth. Who knew how long it would fall through such darkness, fluttering end over end.

The boy watched and waited. He thought at the bottommost point he might sense the plunge of the blade into lifeless silt, into companionship with sundry other items of such provenance. Pistols and pruning shears, medallions of broken promise, skulls newly crowned and arrested newborn, their sockets forever agape with wonder. Among such wreckage his blade would have a home, and some affinity however grotesque and sin-ridden might strike home the notion that he was not alone in the world, not the only one cast out by work of his own hands.

He felt no bottom, no plunge. After a time he pulled himself from the mortared stone rim and looked at the cold brown fields and heaps of snow, the naked trees, and when he walked away the earth beneath him seemed a hollow place where his blade danced ever deeper toward the heart of something black and whole and without end.

His loose-laced boots crunched on the frosted mud road. The road wound over a small rise to the west and toward this he tread, his black slouch hat haloing his head in shadow, the sun rising pale and heatless at his back. He had no pistol, no car. No kin to hide him. None who would. He had only her, his stepsister, no blood between them but what they'd made, and whether she would love him or hate him for what he'd done he could not know. Would not. Her husband's face had looked so surprised at his end, his blood so bright and diffuse against the hard-packed snow.

At the crest of the rise he pulled his coat tighter around his fatless body and looked down a long slope to the next village west. Little houses sat white-roofed with snow. Spires of chimney smoke hung undizzied in their rise from the valley floor, straight as prayers recited at a hearth of warmth and peace. Everything storybook from such height.

He was about to move toward that place when something stopped him. A sound, a rumble out of the east. The way he'd come. He moved quickly off the road and into the trees, grabbing the first broken branch he could to swipe over his tracks. He retreated deeper and deeper into the wood, there being sparse underbrush to hide him. The sound rose rumbling along the road. It was a V8, one in particular. No other motor in this country made a sound like that.

He hid himself best he could behind a slim tree, slim as him, and watched. The car crested the rise and rolled to a stop at the place where he'd just stood. It was the McEvoy car, a '40 Ford in black. The rear end stood much higher than the front, unsprung, no load of shine to set it level. The idle of the engine sounded grumpy, mean, not used to so little throttle.

A McEvoy elder stepped out of the passenger seat and walked to the front of the car, a shotgun cradled in the crook of his arm, a ragged hole at the elbow of his coat.

The bootlegger crouched and examined the road, his hair white beneath his black stovetop hat. He touched the road with two fingers and the boy held his breath to slip nothing from behind his tree. Then the man looked up, right in his direction.

Bridgett had come to him first years ago under an October moon, their parents just married. He was at his father's still a half mile up the mountain from the small cabin where they were all learning to live as one family. She had a fur wrapped over her shoulders against the cold and she appeared out of the hill-slanted trees like a mythic beast of some kind.

"Evening," she said.

"Ain't it past your bedtime?"

"Couldn't sleep. I was wondering could I have a sup of moon. I ain't ever had any."

"Never?"

She shook her head. "Never-ever."

"Well in my experience, it don't put you to sleep. Not till it knocks you flat out."

"I said I couldn't sleep. Not that I wanted to."

"Well."

"Well why not? This is a bootlegging family I been daughtered to, right?"

"Bootleggers run the stuff. What we do is make it."

"And what do you call that?"

He sniffed. "We don't."

"Well, I'll just be going then."

She got up.

"Wait," he said.

He brought the jar from where it sat in the black puddle of darkness between his boots, the liquid cold and moon-silvered in the clear glass, the lightning hidden somewhere in that thick clarity so seemingly without substance or danger or bite.

Her face tightened after the first sip, the white heat in her throat, but she didn't cough or make any sound.

"Goddamn," she said, exhaling.

They passed the jar back and forth between them, the boy showing his palette stoic against the brew. The moon fell slantwise as they drank and slanted they became, the thick liquor glowing whitely at their temples. Before long other starlights rolled over them, alien and leering, and no familiar constellations could be reckoned out of the sky. All had been undone, made liquid, and the world would be recoupled along whatever deviant vectors sought intersection.

Boyd McEvoy was third of five sons, best driver of the lot. So people said, at least. He was not yet thirty with a black beard already struck through with shoots of white when he came for the first time to haul a load for the boy and his father, Old Oldham. The boy did the loading himself, the trunk of the Ford blacker than the surrounding night. Boyd and the boy's father watched side by side, waiting and smoking, and the boy caught Boyd making sideways glances at his stepsister. What he felt was like the scalding flare of moon in his belly.

When Boyd married Bridgett the boy was there in the white chapel, erect and attentive alongside the quartet of McEvoy brothers, all in groomsmen's black. The boy stood on the end, the shortest. Before the service began they slapped each other slyly and mussed one another's hair and whispered jokes magnificently unfit for the Lord's house. But when that wedding song started the procession, they went grim-lipped and serious and the boy, an only child but for Bridgett, welled with awe and envy for the blood that could bound them so tightly, could keep their wilder natures at bay.

The night before the wedding she had come to him at the still for the last time. She had come to say goodbye. She would be moving to Boyd's cabin on McEvoy land, of course. Step-siblings, they had done the thing a last time, no moon to blame, and when she'd left the boy had drunk until the white liquor struck him comatose, sundered from the world, and in the morning he'd woken heaving and sick.

After the wedding he followed everyone down the front steps of the chapel and watched Boyd open the passenger door for his stepsister in her white dress, and she folded the billows neatly underneath her thighs and sat lady-like in that famous Ford. Boyd came around the other side all smiles and cranked the big supercharged motor that had outrun Federal revenuers year after year and drove his bride away, no reason to blame him.

The boy turned away wet-eyed and saw his shadow thrown crazed and misshapen against the church house door.

She started showing four months after the wedding, right on the cusp of suspicion. The boy's father, long sick, passed away a few days later. The widow moved onto McEvoy land to take care of her pregnant daughter. The boy lived on in the once cramped cabin all alone, haunted by shadows and sighs.

When Bridgett's water broke, Boyd was away on a run to Knoxville. A midwife and the girl's mother and assorted McEvoy women were there to deliver the baby. When the head crowned the McEvoy women left the birth room and did not come back.

Bridgett's mother arrived at the small cabin on horseback in the dark stillness before dawn. When the boy opened the door he saw in his stepmother's eyes the rage of all evil afflicted her condensed into a single sin. His own. But when she opened her mouth and told him of the red tuft of hair on the pate of the baby boy, a color conceived from a lineage of dark hairs and blackest the father's, her words shook with fear.

"You," she said. "You of all must do something."

"What?"

"You of all," she said. "You goddamn fool. Boyd will kill it and maybe Bridgett too. You as well. McEvoys do not brook such disgrace."

The boy turned surveying the dim implements cluttered about the cabin.

"The shotgun is up at the still," he said. "I got to get it."

"No time, boy. Boyd will be back sunup from Knoxville."

The boy shook his head and told her to wait a moment and pulled his britches off the bedpost and when he looped his belt he stuck the leather scabbard of his bowie knife through the front. He punched his slouch hat on his head and stove his feet into his boots, no time to lace them.

"Take this here horse," she told him, handing him the reins. "You got to hurry."

He looked up at the horse.

"Yes ma'am," he said.

He took an old horse trail he knew to cut the distance, black spines of ridge and hill limned sheer-edged from the dimmest lightening of dawn. He came down the broken path and intersected the paved road five miles below McEvoy land. He got there just as Boyd's Ford was racketing up the road bug-eyed from the valley below.

The boy broadsided the horse on the road and raised one ungloved hand toward the oncoming car. When it got close the nose and headlights dove toward the pavement, the tires nearly screeching but not.

Boyd hung an elbow out the window, then his black-haired head.

"That you, Oldham's boy?"

"There's been a problem, Boyd."

"With what?"

"With your wife."

Boyd gunned the motor. "Get to the point," he said.

The boy was not sure what point to make. He needed him out of the car.

"Her baby, it ain't yours."

Boyd hung farther out his window.

"Not mine?"

"No, sir."

"Who in the hell's is it then?"

"Mine, I reckon."

The door clicked and swung low and wide and a mustard-colored boot came down on the pavement.

"You reckon, do you?"

He put one big hand on the door and pulled himself out of the car and the boy saw a Colt .45 in his other hand.

"You sick son of a bitch."

"Hold on," said the boy, but Boyd was already leveling the pistol. The boy hauled the horse hard around and slapped her rump hoping Boyd would follow him but what followed was the shot flat and long down the road. The horse faltered, sunk still running to the pavement, and the boy was thrown rolling down the asphalt and off the shoulder into the snow.

The horse screamed somewhere behind him. A second shot silenced her.

"Made me kill one of my horses," said Boyd, standing tall over him. "Maybe that ain't all. This better not be no joke."

"It ain't."

Boyd squatted down low.

"You and me, we're supposed to be brothers now. Brothers-in-law. But sounds like you went and broke that law, didn't you? Just couldn't keep it to yourself. What we got here is a outlaw."

"Like you're the one to say."

"Get up."

The boy did as he was told.

The sun was over the trees, the light strange and gray, the dead horse russet as stillborn fire where the headlights touched her. The road was gunmetal, made crooked by the land, the hills tall and close. Down the pavement a ways an offshoot of dirt wound westward where no great mountain stood. The car idled brokenly behind them. The boy could feel the motor in his chest, the percussions.

He looked at Boyd.

"She's my wife," said Boyd. "And that's my baby in her. So you, you son of a bitch, you won't be coming near her ever again. Understand?"

The boy nodded his head.

"No," he said, "I want to hear you say it. Say you understand."

The boy licked his lips to better pronounce the words, his gaze set past Boyd's shoulder on the mud road west.

"I understand," he said, extending his hand.

When Boyd switched hands to shake the boy pulled the knife.

Afterwards he did not take the pistol, the car. Both scared him, the pistol still clenched in Boyd's hand, the car idling meanly and alien as the engine caged behind his ribs.

The boy turned edgewise the tree to slim his silhouette from the McEvoys on the road. The black bark of the trunk exploded yellow-hearted from the blast and the boy took off running, his hat snagging on a low branch, his progress a crackling of dead limbs, his red hair wild among the black and white wood. Other shots caromed through the trees, each report a relief that the slug had not struck him.

He splashed through a creek clear as moonshine and the water cut right through his loose-laced boots, cold beyond all his reckonings, and it was that ice-couriered clarity more than the shots that told him he would not get cleanly away.

A slug erupted in his hamstring and he fell turning and twisting red-slushed down a long slope toward a broken jaw of black rock upthrust on the verge of a high ridge. He twisted and turned flailing trying to stop his fall and the dirt and stone and root of the land were too slippery and frost-hardened to help him.

He struck the black-toothed crags and felt things crack inside him like all those dead and broken limbs through which he'd plummeted. He opened his eyes and saw his fall red-inked upon the slope above him, and then the stove hats and moon faces of McEvoys appeared on the ridgeline.

He turned from them through jets of pain and saw below him on the valley floor that picture perfect village, the whispers of smoke still unharried by wind or mania, the roofs so white on the neat outlay of shoveled streets.

Kingdom come, maybe, but come not for him.

He turned and saw the line of them still assembling, this family, their hats steepled blackly against the pale sky, their barrels pointing him down like a man being judged.

She and the baby would be safe now, satisfaction given. She could say he forced her. She could say anything.

He turned and pulled himself over the rock edge, turning end over end into the storybook kingdom, his head fire-colored against the slate face of his fall.

THE TATTOOIST'S DAUGHTER

Annie looked at the dime-sized spot of crimson fluid left at the bottom of her mother's glass. Her opportunity.

"That Benson boy has been accepted to medical school," her mother said. "You two used to be so cute together." She paused here as if to await confirmation.

Instead Annie raised her glass and polished off her last inch of wine. She had to catch up.

Her mother rubbed one finger along the rim, thin-edged as a curved knife beneath her fingerprint. Her face blank. "So cute together," she said again. "Of course, who knows what he would think of you"—her eyes drifted to Annie's sleeveless top and exposed arms—"what he would think of you now."

Annie scooped her palm underneath the crystal sphere-shape of her mother's glass, taking the stem between the webbing of her middle fingers. She did the same to her own glass and stood. "More wine?" she asked, smiling.

"There's a merlot in the top right corner of the wine rack."

"You don't want to finish the Cardinal Zin?"

"I think we've had about enough of that, don't you?"

"There's half a bottle left."

"Be a sweetie and open the merlot, please."

"Yes, mother."

On the way into town, Annie had swung by the grocery store to buy a homecoming gift, a bottle of wine. If she drank wine in the city, she drank *red* or *white*, nothing fancy, though she stuck mainly to a marquee concoction of her own design: Jack Rabbit Slim. Jack Daniel's, diet cola, and a dash of white powder. Sometimes the real thing, sometimes not. She had an image to uphold, after all. A business.

But she was coming home and that meant wine. At the grocery store, she'd perused the long shelf of bottles, judging labels one against another. Annie loved the labels, how much art and artifice could be condensed into a 5x7 rectangle of paper. How much identity. The Cardinal Zin bottle offered a manic-sketched debauchee in sacerdotal vestments. His mustaches were straight-inked like Salvador Dali with no playful upturn. Annie had known her mother would hate the bottle. Sacrilege. She'd bought it.

Now she saw it sitting on the kitchen counter alongside the cutting board and the hardening hunk of uncut cheese. She placed the glasses on the counter and thumbed the cork deeper into the zinfandel bottle. When she did, the topless mermaid on the underbelly of her forearm writhed suggestively. The Cardinal stared back at this half-naked specimen lusty-eyed, a kindred djinn of some kind trapped in one dimension just like the tattoo he watched.

"You know," said her mother over the back of the couch, "when you first got here I thought you were wearing long sleeves."

Annie moved Cardinal Zin into the shadows against the wall and slid the bottle of merlot her mother had requested from the rack. "That's what it's called, Mom. A sleeve."

"In this town we call it trash."

Annie looked over her shoulder and saw her mother

sitting primly cross-legged on the couch, her back to her, her face turned in profile to speak better behind her. Her Gucci slipper, gold-buckled, hung expertly from the end of one perfect red-painted big toe. She was not watching Annie. Her head couldn't turn that far around, Annie told herself. Though she didn't put much past the woman.

Annie had her own vices, devices. She reached into her clutch on the counter and removed a caramel-colored pill bottle. Careful not to rattle the pills, Annie removed a benign-looking white tablet. *Mother's little helper*, she thought. That's what the Rolling Stones had called it, their tribute to suburban anti-anxiety prescriptions. She placed the Xanax underneath the heavy glass base and worked the bottle like you would a mortar and pestle, grinding the pill to a white dust on the countertop. She was practiced in this art.

She uncorked the merlot and sloshed their glasses full, took a big pinch of the white powder between her dark-painted fingers and watched the stuff dissolve into the purple elixir of her mother's glass. The sight swelled inside her, thrilling, like a Shakespearean lady poisoning the Queen's chalice, and yet Annie did this for both their goods. Hoping her mother's armor of intolerance, hard-clutched around her as firmly as her bangles and jewelry of gold and chrome, would melt to something liquid, workable. Open to coaxing, persuasion. Shapes formed between them heretofore unknown.

Annie held the glasses underneath her palms again, split-fingered, and walked carefully into the sitting room, eschewing her normal slink for a carriage supremely lady-like, book-balanced, so as not to spill on the rich white silk of the couch or sitting chair. She maneuvered around the piano, sleek and black, on which she could still play Pachelbel's Canon in D Major without the slightest slip of key. No one at the tattoo parlor knew that.

She handed her mother her glass and watched her eye the mermaid tattoo. Her mother drank a sip of the spiked merlot. "Why a mermaid?" she asked, nodding toward Annie's arm.

Annie shrugged. "No reason," she said. The words gargled through a mouthful of wine.

"No reason? I should think a person getting an indelible image imprinted underneath their skin should do so with some smidgen of reason, however specious."

In fact, Annie had reserved that white section of uninked skin for months, deciding what image suited it best. She'd wanted something that spoke to her origins, her arrived state. Then one Saturday, swaddled in a blanket too hungover to move, she'd stumbled onto the Disney channel and watched *The Little Mermaid.* A favorite girlhood movie of hers, Ariel so white-fleshed and innocent, darting through Neptune's depths, and yet woman-bodied even then, perky-breasted and red-haired.

"I wanted something that represented me."

Her mother set the circular base of her glass on the point of her knee, balancing the thin stem between manicured fingers. "You feel represented by a beast of nautical mythology with pointy breasts and a fish-scaled vagina?"

Annie looked at her mother with her tight-tucked jawline, her Yurman necklace in silver and gold inlay perched on her tendoned neck. The crow's feet smoothed from her eyes. Years and experience undone. Her cheeks only slightly reddened from so much wine. This woman adorned in trappings that belied her origins, barefoot in a one-room shack on the Louisiana bayou, her father a shrimper. No gentlemen, no ladies in that place of dirt and roaches and sweat.

Annie took a deep breath. Her power was slipping. She grasped for a hold. "I'm pregnant," she blurted.

Her mother's eyes snapped wide. Tiny red branches of capillaries fractured the whites. For an instant Annie saw in those black pupils the fear that such a grand-babe would be birthed ink-skinned, marked somehow by the prenatal sins of her mother.

Annie looked down at the mermaid's eyes. So bright. Her body had always been to her a thing bold and strong, fearless, the depths of her given rise in script and symbol. Her arms, her chest, the mythology of her soul inked in red and green and black: mermaids and cherry blossoms, jackrabbits and blood-red lotuses. A treasure map inked through sea-monstrous waters and troll bridges. X marks the spot. Her heart. This cartographic skin art had graced the pages of *Prick Magazine*, had put her tattoo studio on the industry map. Always these graphics had adorned her like something ironclad, strong and individualistic and without regret. Leave it to her mother to slip poison into the dye, to make them burn on her skin like the blush of humiliation. Like she'd brought something to light better left hidden, shadowed, denied.

Her mother cleared her throat. "You do know who the father is, I hope?"

"Yes, ma'am. One of my employees."

"Which one?"

"His name is Boy Sunday. He's my best artist."

Her mother nodded, her range of motion perhaps deeper than normal, the medicine going to work. "I should hope so," she said. Then, beyond all Annie's expectations, her mother smiled. Lines creased her face, her eyes, and lipstick clung to the whites of her teeth like a sated vampire.

Annie raised her wine, triumphant. Her mother lunged toward her and blocked the mouth of the glass with a flat, jeweled hand. "You can't be drinking that, Annie Christianson. Not with my grandchild in you."

Annie lowered the glass. "Oh," she said. "Right."

Her mother shook her head back and forth, her eyes closed. "The first trimester," she said. "It's the most important."

Annie placed her glass back on the marble coffee table.

"Good girl," said her mother. Then she gave her knee a slap. "But listen," she said, "we do need to celebrate. You are keeping the baby, aren't you?"

Annie nodded.

Her mother wiggled her tongue against the inside of her lip and nodded. "Let's go get us a couple of ice cream sundaes."

Her eyes were sparkling.

Annie felt something strange in her chest. Something forgotten. She felt it well up inside her like a song.

"Seriously?" she said.

Her mother nodded some more.

"But it's storming outside."

"Damn the weather." Her mother bolted upright and tottered, surveying the room squint-eyed. "My keys," she said.

"We'll go in my car," said Annie. "If I got to be sober I might as well drive."

They dashed to Annie's car through driving rain that silvered in the garage lights. Once inside, she hit the red START button.

"Where's the key?" asked her mother.

"You don't need one. It'll start as long as you've got this fob within a few feet of the car."

"Shit, that's fancy," said her mother. Annie could not remember having ever heard her mother swear.

There was an old-school ice cream parlor several blocks away. Annie drove toward it on the slick black streets, dodging fallen branches that reared out of the darkness beyond the long racy hood of the sports car. The windows of the place were white with light, chrome trim sparkling behind them. Pimply boys sulked behind the counter in paper hats and aprons. Annie felt their eyes crawl her skin when she walked inside, reading the signs and wonders and contours that defined her. They straightened. Annie felt the old empowerment returning, the wonder, and when their eyes climbed all the way to her own they looked away, awestruck, wiping the sparkling countertop with their rags. It didn't hurt that she was pretty.

Her mother sat her purse on the counter. "I would like an ice cream cone, French vanilla."

"Single scoop?" asked the boy.

She lowered her head to him, a sly grin on her face.

"*Double*," she said.

"I thought you were getting a sundae, mother."

"Nope. French vanilla is all I need."

Annie looked at the glass window that divided her from the many-colored buckets of swirled ice cream, the toppings. She looked at the nearest server. "Didn't you used to be able to do your own toppings here?"

He nodded hurriedly. "I heard it used to be like that. Apparently people was going overboard, cutting into profit margins and all."

"Is your manager here?"

"No, ma'am. But I'd be happy to get you whatever you'd like."

"Would you let me make my own sundae?"

The boy looked at his compatriot, then the mean weather outside. "I guess it couldn't hurt," he said. Annie hopped onto the counter and spun around on her butt until her long legs reached the employee side.

"Why Annie…" said her mother. Then she tapped her finger on the nearest boy's shoulder and leaned toward his ear, conspiratorial. "She always was wild," she told him.

Annie started with two snow-white scoops of regular vanilla, perfectly round. Then she moved expertly down the line of toppings and syrups, her hands working the ladles and serving spoons with practiced deftness, cross-lacing creamy hills with caramel and chocolate ribbons, rocking the surface with black crags of broken cookie, confetti-ing hilltops with party-colored sprinkles. Once she looked up and saw her mother watching wide-eyed, slack-jawed, a dim light of understanding in her look. "She used to do this as a child," she told the boy at the register. "She'd spend ten minutes decorating her sundae and twenty minutes eating it. She wouldn't eat it plain."

When Annie finished she sat cross-legged on the stainless countertop and ate her sundae with an extra long spoon. Her mother sat on a stool. The boys tried to busy themselves with cleanup, but not a single crumb marred the glance of light off the steel lip of the toppings line. Annie took little snippets from the hillsides, deconstructing her design by slight degrees. Outside their little parlor, the night was dark, but moments of lightning matched the brilliance of the sky to that of their well-lighted place.

By the time they got back in the car, Annie saw her mother's head lolling slightly with the wine, the medicine, the French vanilla ice cream. A queer feeling turned over in her stomach. Guilt. Her mother reached over and pressed the tab of her finger into the underbelly of Annie's arm, the mermaid.

"You used to love the mermaid in that little Disney movie, remember that?"

"I do. I do remember that."

Her mother kept her finger pressed there into her arm, her weight shifting toward Annie, her posture wilting with exhaustion. When she parted her lips to speak, Annie could hear the dry smack of her tongue and gums, cottonmouth they called it, and her words came in a low, intimate slur: "Do you want a boy or a girl, Annie?"

Annie felt her eyes welling, her vision matching the blurred world beyond the windshield. She took a long moment to decide what to say.

"I want a daughter," she said.

When she looked at her mother, her eyes had closed, her mouth mashed slackly against the bolster of the leather seat. She seemed to nod so slowly Annie did not know whether she nodded at all.

That night Annie lay awake a long time in the dark blueness of her old room, feeling welcome here, even home. But the tiny white seed inside her, the one she'd sown herself, threatened to spoil everything, to grow fierce and blinding, tentacled, an alien thing that might blot out this place, these quilts, a mother's hand on her arm. There was a thing inside her she could not affirm in ink. She did not want to own it, this thing she'd done.

In the morning she awoke to light coming slantwise through her window. She stood, pulled on her jeans, tied her sneakers. She pulled her hair into a tight ponytail and brushed her teeth. She could hear her mother in the kitchen as she descended the stairs, dishes clanking and the sizzle of fat on a burner. Her mother was standing before the stove in workout clothes, one bare foot rested on the other, one elbow cupped in her palm. A spatula held limp-wristed in her hand. She did not turn around when Annie's sneakers creaked along the white tiles.

"I'm making turkey sausage and egg whites," she said.

"That's okay," said Annie. "I don't eat breakfast."

Instead she poured a cup of coffee from the pot and sat on a stool to drink it, watching her mother in profile. The bottle of Cardinal Zin sat on the counter between them. The label had been turned toward the wall. Annie let the coffee scald her throat. "I had a good time last night," she said.

"That's good," said her mother. "I've got a yoga class at ten.

You really should eat breakfast." She jabbed the sausages around the pan with quick, dart-like movements.

"Aren't you going to eat breakfast?" asked Annie.

Her mother shook her head. "No, I've got to burn off the calories."

"The calories from what?"

"From the, the—"

"From the what, Mom?"

Her mother shook her head. Silent. Annie felt her hand tighten on the coffee mug. It felt fragile, crushable.

"From the ice cream?"

Her mother nodded, not saying "the ice cream." For some reason Annie had wanted her to say it. Needed her to. And when she didn't, Annie felt the thing going mean inside her, hurt. Denied. She gripped the mug harder.

"Going to get ice cream was just so much fun last night, wasn't it?"

Her mother turned her head but didn't see her, looking instead at the tides of ink risen along her exposed neck.

"What in God's name is *that*?" she asked, pointing with the greased fin of the spatula. Annie ran her finger along the dotted trace of the treasure map where it rose from her shoulder traversing the blue pool of a sea monster tattooed on the low side of her neck.

"It's a treasure map," she said. She pulled down the collar of her shirt and turned her head to display this region of the map in further detail. "After this it tracks southward, toward my heart."

"Oh my God," said her mother. "You mean you've tattooed…your chest?"

"Some of it."

"Why would you do that to yourself, Annie? For God's sake, what if, what if the dye infects your milk?"

Many women had asked Annie the same question before

getting their tattoos, and yet coming from this quarter it infuriated her, the inferior question to a thousand others that she wanted her mother to ask: names and fathers, schools, who might have unburied that treasure in her chest.

"Why would you ask me that, Mother? Of course it won't infect the milk. Of course I know that. I'm a tattoo artist, for God's sake. I'm *the* tattoo artist in the city."

Her mother waved the spatula at her. "They didn't call them artists in my day. Just tattooists, plain and simple. No art about it."

"Well maybe your day is over then, Mother."

"Maybe you should watch your mouth, little girl. I can't believe someone of your maturity level is going to have a little girl. God help her."

Annie felt the thing inside her kick for the surface and she clamped one hand over her mouth. In the other hand she gathered up her keys, her purse, and in a whelm of spite she grabbed the Cardinal Zin bottle from against the wall.

Her mother put one hand on her hip. "So that's it? You're just running away now?"

The thing burst out of Annie's throat.

"I'm not, Mother."

"Not running?"

"I'm not having a little girl, or a little boy, or any baby at all. It was a lie. All of it was a lie."

Annie watched her mother's spirit dwindle, saw it in her face. The dead nerves, the dry constriction of her throat.

"How could you, Annie?"

Annie spat the words: "So you'd love me."

Her cheeks were flushed, her eyes burned. She turned to run back to her car, her city, her studio. Her mother reached for her as she turned and her clawed hand snagged the bottle instead, ripping it from the crook of Annie's arm. It wheeled into the air between them, heavy and leering.

Both of them dropped to their knees to catch it, but the bottle fell right between their outstretched hands and burst on the white tile at their feet, a deep red hemorrhage of glass and fluid that covered them both. Their feet, their knees, their hands.

BONE VALLEY

Hart stood on the wooden platform, alone, the blackwater churning beneath him. The gator pit. His lasso circled above him, flecks of moisture haloing the rope in orbital rings, the stage lights angled just-so for the effect. He watched a good-looking reptile come beating its way through its peers. No scars on him, no mutilations. You needed a handsome gator for a show. The young and mean were best. The ones with something to prove.

Hart dropped the lariat from showboating altitude. The gator's jaws yawned wide at him. A pink mouth, eighty-odd teeth snaggled and underbit. Smiling or killing, all the same. Hart roped him, noosed the neck. The reptile hissed and rolled, its pale belly surfacing once, twice. Hart dragged him onto the platform. He straddled the ridged back, kneeling, the cold blood soft between his thighs. He vised the jaws shut with big-knuckled hands, meaty palms. Another handler stepped in to bind the mouth. They carried the animal out of the enclosure, walking him amid the pens of nonworking gators. People could watch the wrangling out here, in the corrals, but no one did, not for years. The only show was in the sand pit, what show there was.

In the pit: he ground his boots in the sand, readying

himself. They cut the gator loose. It came at him, fat belly slithering through the trapdoor. Hart got round the side of him, quickly, and dropped to his knees. He pried open the jaws and stuck his head inside the open mouth. His first stunt. The stench was foul, old. He turned to look at the grandstands from inside those yellow-jagged teeth, smiling his own yellow smile, his silver cap on one tooth glinting in the stage light.

The stands were nearly empty. There was a little girl with a pink plume of cotton candy in one hand, the wrist of a grandmother who was looking skyward, lost, in the other. This moment lingered an instant too long. The alligator bit down. Hart yanked his head away, out, a crooked tooth catching the bare pate of his scalp. He got his hands away from the teeth before the jaws snapped shut, a thin seam of blood already tickling the side of his skull. He locked the mouth shut and tilted his head to keep the blood out of his eye.

His backup, a boy of twenty-five with diluted Seminole blood, leaned forward and hula-ed a roll of duct tape on the end of his finger. He had his sleeves rolled high to show off his beach muscles, but his grip was weak. Hart thought it would cost him a hand, had said as much to the pit manager. Everyone just shrugged.

"You ought to tape him," said the boy. "Save him for a bigger show."

Hart shook his head. You were supposed to run your scheduled shows whether there were spectators or not. He slipped back to straddling the gator's back and continued his repertoire of tricks. The Florida Smile, the Bulldog, the Face-Off. His chin resting lightly on the gator's snout, his arms thrown outward and winglike, the reptile's jaws gaped pinkly and hot underneath his face.

The little girl threw her hands over her mouth, in awe.

~ ~ ~

They said there were gator parks popping up across the West, in Colorado especially. Ones that paid good, that didn't treat you like another piece of meat. That didn't hope you'd screw up and make news losing a hand or worse, boosting ticket sales.

This is what he thought about as he walked out to his truck in the employee lot. He did not walk so much as waddle, his knees crackling, his knuckles aching, his forearms engorged from the day's labor. His tattoos warped and muddled by too much blood and sun. He was fifty-eight years old.

On the drive home he envisioned great mountains rising above the beachfront condos and gated townhomes, the department stores and box restaurants, the check-cashing places and pawn shops. He envisioned them rising jagged against the sky, like teeth, their summits snow-swept and treeless, the snow bright and cold in the sun.

He blinked and the vision was gone. The sky was an ocean, violet, empty but for the tiny jeweled lights of airliners winking in the dusk.

He stopped at a 7/11 and bought a six-pack of Coors. He sat in his big green corduroy recliner and let them run cold down his throat, his eyes squinted unseeing at the snowy screen beneath the bunny-ears of his TV antenna. When he was finished, before bed, he snipped the six holes of the plastic soda binder with a pair of scissors he kept in a drawer by his chair. The sea turtles, they could be strangled in the hoops.

Sundays he drove inland to the phosphate mines. He hunted the spoil piles of washed overburden. He hunted the slurry pits. The crews were gone. The quarries were like enormous craters on the moon, white-blasted and barren. The mining equipment strange and silent as the abandonments of spacemen.

This was the seafloor of prehistory. Sea monsters swam through what was now the sky. This land was a land of bones. The fossil bed lay twenty to forty feet under an unknowing populace. Shells and skeletons of fallen sealife had accrued for eons, for time so long that even man, with his highly developed brain, his short-lived ego, could not comprehend. Only exploit. Twenty-five percent of the world's supply came from this phosphate. Bone Valley, it was called.

Hart would come home with giant shark's teeth, some the size of a dinner plate. They were black. He would come home with three-toed horse teeth, shell fragments of giant tortoises, a few arrowheads. He would never come home empty-handed.

These treasures from the phosphate mines, he sent them to Colorado, to the last known address he had for his son. Six years old, his son had wanted to be an archaeologist, to unearth creatures heretofore unknown.

Hart wrapped the teeth and bones in bubble wrap, he packed them in manila envelopes. These calcium remains of periods past, species gone. He sent them first-class. He had to remember to write the address on the envelope before he packed it. Otherwise, his writing would be jagged and uneven.

His son would be twenty-eight years old this October.

His phone rang just after midnight. He rolled over in bed and found the receiver.

"Yeah?"

"Hart? It's Bo Sherman with the FWC."

"Shit."

"I know," said Bo. "You got something to write on?"

Hart fetched his reading glasses out of the side-table drawer along with a pen. No paper. He held the ballpoint to his open palm.

"Lemme have it," he said.

"Two-oh-one Landon Drive," said Bo.

"Uh-huh. Got it."

"And Hart, I need you to make trails on this one. It's got somebody's arm." The Fish & Wildlife officer paused a moment. "A kid's," he said.

"Don't dare let them sharpshooters at it."

"I'm trying," said Bo. "Just get your ass over here."

"I will."

His truck was packed with everything he needed for wrangling, his moonlight job. The Fish & Wildlife boys called him when an alligator turned up where it shouldn't, in a country club pond or somebody's backyard. When they needed it brought in, and quick.

He steered with his knees as he buttoned his shirt. At 201 Landon Drive he jabbed the brakes. The drive had taken twelve minutes. On the way he'd watched a medivac helicopter blink across the sky. Headed toward Tampa General, most likely.

He threw the truck into park amid the police cruisers and FWC pickups. They were all empty, their light-bars whirling silently under the oaks. The house was an aged neo-classic behemoth with unruly vines spiraling its columns, kudzu rampant on the lot. He fetched his go-bag from the truckbed and hurried around the house and through the foot-high backyard and down the embankment to where a half circle of men in uniform had congregated at pond's edge. FWC officers in khaki, sheriffs in green, city cops in navy.

In their middle was an officer in black garb with a scoped

bolt-action rifle steadied on the back of an ATV. It had the heavy sniper's barrel, and he was aiming it toward the middle of the pond. He was wearing a ballcap backwards that read: SWAT. The moon was up, nearly full, but visibility across the water was low, ripples silvering across the black surface of the pond.

He ran faster, straight toward the marksman.

"No," he said. "Don't shoot!"

He stumbled on a root and crashed to the ground amid the wildlife officers and sheriffs at water's edge. When he got up he was covered in blood. The victim's. He was shaking his head.

"Don't," he said.

The officers stood back. The SWAT man turned his head slowly toward him. He had a square jaw and golden skin. "You want to shut up?" he asked. "I got a shot to make."

Hart started toward the man. Bo Sherman tried to stop him. He pushed past.

"Oh no you don't," Hart said. "You don't have the visibility, the angle either. You miss by a quarter inch and that gator'll be under for forty-five, fifty minutes."

"Then I won't miss."

Hart looked to his side. Two paramedics were standing by with a biovac cooler filled with ice. It was starting to melt. He turned back to the SWAT officer.

"You can't do this," he said.

Bo Sherman came up and touched his arm.

"It's not your call, Hart. I'm afraid the decision's been made."

Hart didn't move.

The SWAT officer jutted his chin toward him. "Can somebody get this civ outta here, please? Jesus." He shook his head and went back to his scope, his left eye mashed up to aim.

Bo tightened his grip on Hart's arm.

"Let's go," he whispered. Hart conceded. Bo guided him a few feet back from the scene, coaxing him gently like you would some large and obstinate animal.

The SWAT sniper let off his shot. They watched a silver geyser erupt on the pond's surface. A miss. The black head of the gator slipped underneath the surface.

Hart unzipped his go-bag and got out his throw-lines, the ones with the custom-brazed treble hooks.

"Let's get me in that Zodiac," he said, nodding to the inflatable boat sitting by pond's edge on a set of rollers. "We'll wait for him to come back up."

Bo Sherman nodded.

The SWAT officer was breaking down his weapon as they readied the boat. The big muscles of his arms rippled and contracted visibly as he detached the bipod, capped the scope, latched the case. Finally he came over.

"Might of made that shot you hadn't got in my head."

"Get your finger out of my face," said Hart.

"You old son of a—"

Hart caught him under the chin with an open palm and put him down across the back of the ATV. He clamped down on the man's throat. It was soft and compliant in his hand, weak. There were yells that hardly reached him, coming as if from a long way off. Then blows across his back, his arms. A white tongue of power ripped through his body. He blinked and found himself on the ground, dazed, the blood at water's edge creeping coolly through the seat of his shorts. He saw the blue jag of electricity coming again for him. A taser. A cop's.

Bo Sherman knocked it away.

Hart struggled to his feet. The city cops were rabid now. They wanted him arrested. They had their stunguns and batons out.

"Not if you want that little girl's arm back you don't," said Bo Sherman. The other Fish & Wildlife officers stood behind him, arms crossed.

They chugged out to the middle of the pond. Hart stood in the front of the boat.

"How'd it happen?" he asked.

Bo Sherman leaned forward from the throttle. "Son of a bitch couldn't keep his mouth shut, I reckon—"

"I mean the attack."

"Oh," said Bo. "Little girl's dog went missing earlier this evening. You can imagine who done it. She was down in the shallows, looking for him in the reeds. Grandma called. Said it'd got her arm. Told the dispatcher it was something prehistoric, apparently. Sarc, Sarco-something."

"Sarcosuchus," said Hart. He had a treble-hooked line hanging low over the water in one hand. "SuperCroc. Probably saw it on *60 Minutes*. Big as a city bus."

"Let's hope not."

"Yeah," said Hart. "Let's."

The gator resurfaced sixty-five minutes later. Hart had never seen one stay under so long. These were air-breathers, after all, and must hold their breath.

The head was massive, like a giant floating log. He hooked the pale belly with an underhanded throw. This was how the Cajuns did it when they did it in open water. Bo Sherman made the shot. The bullet severed the brainstem at the base of the skull. Bo did not use his service pistol. He used a short-barreled .22 rifle that Hart kept in his go-bag. Less paperwork, he said. The gator was twelve feet, easy.

They beached the Zodiac and rolled the reptile over the side. Hart kneeled and gutted the belly with a hooked knife. The paramedics gave him plastic gloves before he reached into the stomach. He dug into the great lizard's innards. He found the dog first, a chihuahua it looked like. He kept digging. Through fur, slime, undigested teeth and bone.

Up came the arm. It was ghostly pale, lifeless, like the special-effects prop from a slasher film. Strange, inhuman. The bloody stump held a white stab of bone. He held it by the forearm, so tiny. His pressure on the tendons made the fingers move. On one of the fingers was a plastic gumball machine ring in the shape of a butterfly. It looked like a moth now, no longer bright.

He knew that ring.

The paramedics cast the ring aside and placed the arm in the bed of ice and zipped the cooler closed. They had already been on the radio. You could hear the medivac chopper setting down in a church parking lot a block distant. They hurried off to deliver the limb.

Hart cleaned and packed his gutting tools and throw-lines. No one spoke. It had taken too long. The tissue of the limb would be dead by now. Too long cut off from the heart, little hope for reattachment. Everyone knew it. Bo Sherman patted him on the shoulder and shook his head, silent.

As he walked to his truck he saw the SWAT officer leaning on an unmarked cruiser. He was smoking a cigarette. Hart could see the shadow of his own hand blooming darkly upon the man's neck. The officer picked something off his tongue and flicked it away and stared at his boots. Hart dropped his go-bag into the bed. He turned around. Two city cops were standing by the door of his truck, their handcuffs out.

He was six hours in the holding cell. Beside him slumped a drunk, snoring, his beard stiffened by vomit. Across from him a young man with no shirt, his body inked with tattoos like a skin-tight suit. The designs reached up his neck and under his chin. He was staring down at his open hands, as if they had betrayed him.

Hart was not charged. He could thank Bo Sherman for that, most likely. Dawn was just breaking when the heavy metal door clicked shut behind him. He was standing in a parking lot. The razor-wire fence was open for him. How many sobered degenerates had shuffled into daylight this way, wishing they could crawl back into the darkness?

His truck had been impounded. He didn't have the cash to get it back. He thought about using his credit card, if they allowed it. He didn't want to put anything more on credit. He was supposed to be at the park in two hours. That was east from here. He could make it if he started now.

He started walking west.

He walked until the buildings grew taller, newer. The people parted before him, before this bloodied hulk. They switched their suitcases to the outside hand, they moved toward the street. He crossed a short bridge. Tampa General rose before him. There was a chopper on the helipad, its rotors wilted and still. He walked through the sliding glass doors. It was cool and clean indoors. He drank a cup of complimentary coffee in the lobby. A news crew arrived a half hour later. The first of many, he expected. They would know the room number.

He followed them into the elevator and got off on the same floor they did. The crew headed purposefully down the hallway. A reporter, a cameraman, a producer. Hart saw a nurse coming from the other direction, ready to intercept.

His moment.

He got in front of the news crew and threw out his arms. His shirt was still crusted with dried blood, and his eyes were wild.

"The family doesn't want to see you," he said. "Not now."

They stuck a microphone in his face.

"Can you tell us your relationship to the victim?"

Hart noticed the nurse standing next to him now.

"Her grandfather," he lied.

The nurse led him to the room. She opened the door for him and shut it behind him, a gentle click. The girl was asleep, her body swaddled in bandages and fed by tubes, her life charted by colored graphs. The old woman was sitting by the bed. She looked up at him.

"You," she said.

He dipped his head. "Ma'am."

"You," she said. "*You.*"

"Yes ma'am."

"Monsters," she said. There was conviction in her eyes. A crazed conviction. "Monsters all." She began to tremble and shake. Her hands writhed in her lap. "God damn them," she said. "They should kill them off. *Extinct.*"

"No," he said.

"No? No?" She looked at him, her mouth agape. "You make of them toys," she said. "Playthings." She leaned forward and hugged herself, as if someone had punched her in the gut. "Why weren't you there to protect her? You or someone like you. Off showboating, when you ought to be hunting them down, every last one."

He knew how she saw him then. A link to another world. To the violence that lay sleeping underneath the sidewalks, the neatly-painted streets and four-lane superhighways, the fiberglass hulls and bermuda grass lawns. The violence that was never really asleep. She thought that he could wrangle it. Could bend it to his will. That it could be bent.

He walked over to the steel sink and pulled something out of his pocket. He washed it with soap and scalding water.

He walked back to the old woman. He felt he could say anything. He squatted down before her and put the butterfly ring into one of her palms. Her wrists were thin, her veins blue. He closed her fingers over the treasure. He held her hands.

"You tell her not to be afraid," he said. "You tell her this was not evil that done this to her. Not a monster. You make sure it don't ruin her, you hear me?"

The old woman's eyes were wide. She seemed to be listening.

"You tell her not to be afraid. She is, you take her to come see me."

He stood and looked down at the little girl, the empty space where her arm should be.

"Yes," said the old woman, her eyes lost somewhere. "Yes."

Hart stood outside on the sidewalk. The side of the hospital glowed brightly, glass spangled by a dozen mirrored suns. He turned and looked west. He felt that if he were to squint hard enough, long enough, he might just make out those distant ranges, the treeless granite serrating the sky, the rising sun scrawled in ragged traces across all that nakedness, as upon a prehistoric world.

He turned and walked east, toward home. Hobbling. His bones grinding in their sockets, his architecture stubborn, unbroken.

THE VIZSLA

His father was a breeder of gun dogs. Pointers, wire-haired, enlivened the fields before him like some vanguard of old. The dogs stepped lightly through the tall grasses. Their ears were flung outward like small wings, their heads cocked. Their noses ever-twitching, telling them secrets he would never know. He cradled his shotgun close against his chest. He watched them work. He was sixteen years old.

They flushed a covey of game-birds, doves, from a tall thicket of scrub-grass. The birds exploded from the roost, panicked and whistling, and he shot two of them black against the blue sky. Their wings folded against their bodies and they tumbled from the air. The dogs retrieved them, soft-jawed and light-eyed. One of the birds was still alive, twitching. He twisted its neck until it cracked.

The light was dying when they crested the last hill toward home. The dogs were slinking a little, tired and hungry. Him too. He put them in their kennels and fed them. They each ate separate. He slid the bowls through slots in the chain-link. He called them *boy* or *girl,* depending. He rarely called them by their names. He was not the one who named them.

The last light retreated into the horizon. He leaned against the old willow and smoked a cigarette. From here he could see the yellow rectangle of light, the kitchen window. He could see his father in there, in his overalls. He could see him fishing in the fridge for a new beer. When he stood up straight, beer in hand, his head was right in the crosshairs of the windowpanes.

The screen door banged shut behind him. His father was sitting in his recliner, as always. A can of Budweiser sweating in his palm. He did not turn around to look.

"You feed 'em?"

"Yes sir."

"Drizzle on some that fish oil, like I told you?"

"Yes sir."

"You get dinner?"

The boy set his game-bag on the kitchen table.

"Good," said his father. "Better get cooking. I'm starving."

The boy cut a block of butter into a glass dish and turned on the oven.

"Yes sir," he said.

They ate oven-fried dove on white plates with sauteed peas. His father did not look at his dinner. He looked at the television set. The dark pearls of lead shot from the meat, he set them in a tight grouping on the oilcloth table setting. The boy spat his into a wastebasket he'd set near his foot. They ate in silence. On TV, Clint Eastwood sat his horse, squinting. The old set made his skin look orange, the mountains purple.

"Can I borrow the truck tonight?"

The old man sniffed.

"What for?"

"Just to get out."

"Skylarking. Waste of time and money."

The boy said nothing. He looked at the television set and spat a nugget of lead into the wastebasket.

His father was asleep in his recliner, his mouth a black vent that dribbled moisture. On TV, Clint peeled away his poncho, revealing an iron shield. The boy wondered why nobody had aimed for his head. He slipped out the backdoor and opened the truck door and set the gearshift into neutral. He began rolling the truck down the gravel drive, toward the road.

He cranked the engine a safe distance from the house and headed for the old railroad bridge. The moon was puddled in the dark slink of the river. The stars were out. No clouds. The boys were already on the bridge. Ricco and Troy, Danny and Sal. He could see them sitting up there, their silhouettes huddled against the night sky like dark and enormous birds. They had a case of beer, begged or stolen. The cans were silver. They threw him one as he approached.

"You're just in time," said Ricco.

"For what?"

Ricco handed him a rifle. "You know what."

He sat down next to Troy and propped the rifle on his thigh.

Troy looked over at him. "You're dead," he said.

Whit spat.

Ricco pointed at Troy. "You ready?"

"Sure am."

He pointed at Whit. "You?"

Whit nodded.

"Three, two, one, go!"

Whit and Troy popped their beers and started chugging. Troy finished first. He jumped up, hopped the railroad tracks, and hurled the empty can over the far side of the bridge. Then he jumped back, propped his rifle against one of the bridge's steel trusses, and thumbed off the safety. He had a fancy autoloader chambered for .308. When the can appeared from under the bridge, sliding downstream, he started shooting. Geysers shot up around it.

"Shit," he said. "Shit."

Whit was right behind him. He was slower, smoother. The rifle they'd given him was an old bolt-action .22. When his own empty can appeared, he shot once. A black gape; it started to sink.

"Shit," said Troy, differently this time. He sat down and groped in the box for another beer.

Whit sat down next to Ricco, handed him the rifle.

Ricco leaned over and bumped him, shoulder to shoulder.

"What'd you get into today, bud?"

Whit cracked a new beer and shrugged. "Went out running a couple of the old man's dogs is all."

Troy leaned forward.

"You run that dog for my Daddy?"

"Maybe."

"He says he didn't pay for no dog trained by you. Says your Daddy better make sure she's good-to-go, or he ain't paying."

"He'll pay," said Whit.

"You sound pretty sure," said Troy.

"I am."

Whit felt his way back to the truck. Clouds had moved in; he could hardly see. His feet were unsteady, his vision liquid. The other boys were staying longer. It was Friday. He had to be up early tomorrow for chores.

The first beer can hit him dead in the gut as he came through the backdoor. It was full. He dropped to his knees and covered his face. The second beer, a Budweiser, busted his hand against his head. He turned and scrambled through the screen door and rolled down the back stoop.

"I told you not to take my truck, you little son of a bitch!"

A third beer struck the doorframe, hemorrhaging foam.

"Out drinking, that it? Here, have another!"

The last beer tore the screen from the door. Whit was already clawing his way up the back slope toward the kennels, clutching his bruised hand to his chest. He got to the chain-link door of the first one. A wire-haired vizsla, Sarah. He fumbled for his keys. He looked over his shoulder. His father's shadow filled the rectangular light of the backdoor a moment, then started down the back steps, a case of beer under his arm. Whit got the padlock undone and crawled through the dog-sized door in the chain-link.

The vizsla had been curled in a ball; she had her head up now, watching him. Her eyes were almond, white-rimmed with alarm. Her ears were perked. She jumped up and came to him, sniffing him, her nose light against his skin. Inspecting him for wounds, for blood.

His father stood lopsidedly at the fence. Whit could smell him.

"Come out of there, you little son of a bitch!"

Whit held his hand to his chest, said nothing. The dog stood looking at the old man, rigid. His father grabbed hold of the chain-link and rattled it, violently.

"You hear me, you little—"

The dog exploded with fury, snarling, her wolf-teeth bared, her ears back.

"No!" said Whit.

He reached out to the dog, to pull her to safety. She was whelmed with power, quivering. He got her by the haunches. He was afraid what his father might do. But when he looked up, his father had stepped back from the fence. There was something strange in the old man's face: surprise. He turned and staggered slowly back to the house.

Dawn. The sky was red, like a fire just over the horizon. He rose stiffly from the concrete floor. The vizsla looked up from her bed. Her head was cocked at him, her eyes wide, as if asking him a question.

"Good girl," he told her.

He ruffled the scruff under her chin. Then he unlocked the padlock from inside the kennel and crawled through the door. The lights in the house were already on. He could see his father moving in the kitchen. He walked through the back door. His father's hair was slicked back, clean. His overalls were pressed. He was cooking breakfast.

"Morning," he said.

Whit said nothing.

"I'm cooking breakfast."

"I saw."

They sat at the table. Eggs, sunny-sided, and microwave sausage patties. Whit was hungry but forked his food around the plate.

"Last night—" said his father.

"Let's not talk about it," said Whit.

This was not the first time, not the last.

"But this time—" said his father.

Whit got up and walked to the bathroom and turned on the shower.

The phone rang. Whit was just in from feeding the dogs. The sun had just cleared the trees. His father answered.

"Parker's Gun Dogs," he said. He listened.

"Sarah, you say?" He shot a quick glance at Whit. Whit gave him no indication. "Sure," said his father. "She's ready."

~ ~ ~

They pulled up an hour later, Troy and his father. They drove a big Dodge, black, with camouflaged rocker trim. It had metal dog-boxes in the bed and a whip antenna steadied with a tennis ball. Troy had on his hunting bib, blaze orange. He had a dip in. He spat in the driveway while his father rubbed his hands together and asked to see his new vizsla.

"We wanna run her this morning," he said. "Get us some quail."

"You won't be disappointed," said Whit's father.

When they left, Whit went to clean out the empty kennel. He removed the plaid bed and dog bowls. He swept it out and hosed it down. The other dogs watched him, nervous. When he went inside his father was depositing the cash in the small safe in his office. Whit went to the freezer and got a frozen pack of peas. He needed to ice his hand.

It was noon when the Dodge returned, rattling down their drive at speed. It bounced over the red ruts and skidded to a stop. Whit was standing on the jump-dock, launching deadfowl dummies for a pair of German short-hairs they were training. He quickly ordered them back to their pens. He locked them up and turned around in time to see Troy jump from the truck on one side, his father from the other. They left the doors open. His father dropped the tailgate and grabbed a dog by its collar and slid it out of the bed. It dropped slackly to the dirt. It was the vizsla, Sarah. Troy's father stood over the body, hands on his hips. Looking at the house. Troy reached in through the passenger side and honked. Whit wanted for something scoped. He would have used it.

His father came ambling out of the house. His face was red. Whit started down the hill, fast. The shouting had started, the finger-pointing. He went straight to the dog.

Her front leg was bent strangely, like it had an extra joint. A red shard was visible at the break. Blood pooled on the ground. Her head lay on the ground, her one eye watching all this. Whit looked into it. In its wet orb he saw the shadowy violence reflected, the boot-stamping and black-mouthed curses. He turned around.

"Goddamn bitch bit me," said Troy's father. He held out his arm. It was neatly vented at the forearm, red punctures crowned in bruise. The man's mouth was wet.

"How'd she break that leg?" asked Whit's father.

Troy sniffed. "Daddy kicked the bitch for biting him," he said. "That's how."

"You're damn right I did. Put her down is what I should of done."

Whit's father looked at the two men. Then he looked at Whit, sideways. Something flickered in his eyes: light.

"Well," he said. "She never did like assholes."

Troy's father hit him in the jaw with a closed fist. You could hear the crack. Whit's father went down to his knees, and the man hit him again, again. He held him by his shirt so he couldn't go down. Whit's father turned his head. His mouth and chin were messy and wet, his face bright-bearded with blood. His nose bubbled. His teeth were red. Troy's father hit him again.

Whit looked at Troy. The boy leaned and spat. Smirked. Whit leapt across and feinted a punch. Troy covered. Whit kneed him in the groin. The boy dropped, face twisted with pain. Troy's father had a pistol holstered at the small of his back. A fancy nickel-plated Colt with trick grips. It wiggled when he punched. Whit looked at it a long moment. Then he looked at his father, his face purpled and leaking. His jaw slack, like he was laughing. This man beating him, he was not going to stop. He was breathing hard. His face was flushed. But you could see it in his eyes. He wanted blood.

Whit reached over and ripped the gun from its holster. He worked the slide and fired a round off into the sky.

Everything stopped.

"Get off him."

The man dropped Whit's father. He pulled his son off the ground. The two of them walked backwards to their truck, slowly.

"You little son of a bitch," he said. "You'll pay for this. The both of you will."

"Maybe," said Whit.

They tore off down the drive in a fit of smoke. Whit watched them a long time. He wanted to make sure they were gone. The truck disappeared down the far bend. He decocked the pistol and turned around. His father was not where he'd been. The ground was red-streaked where he'd crawled. He was curled next to the whimpering dog. He was whispering to her. Petting her.

"Good girl," he was telling her. "You're a good girl. We'll get you fixed up, I promise."

Whit stood over them. Their blood was mixed in the dirt. His father's. The dog's. The red earth darkened like molasses. His father looked up. The old man's face was monstrous, misshapen, a storm of bruise and blood. But his eyes, they rose wide-welled and quivering from the damaged flesh. Hoping. Pleading. Not for help. For something else. Something harder to give.

Whit looked down at him a long moment. He worked his jaws. Blinked. He looked away. He started inside to call the vet. To get his father the bag of peas.

BLACK SWAN

She started over with one out of three sons and a buried pile of sweet potatoes. The other two of each were scorched, litter and staple both. Gunpowder and flambeau had rent a scar across the republic, clay and flesh red-gaped. Her heart hardened to a fist.

A month after the march, two night riders debouched from the wood to have their way, hungry and carnal. Confederates. Tied him, her lone remaining, to an amputee oak and cornered her in the burnt pantry. She soul-mined them both, armed with shears. Never so much blood, it came black as Texas crude. She put them in the ground, caparisoned in soot-streaked grays, teeth yellowed. Her lone remaining, a boy full of shrapnel, dug a two-man grave in the soft spot where the sweet potatoes had been. She dropped her crusted shears into the yawning earth beside them, story thus entombed.

A century later, great-grandson Winston was born disfigured, his feet curled club-like, purple and mean as twin bludgeons. But the orthopedists un-contorted his destiny in the modern fashion. Staples, pins, and fasteners riveted conformity from malleable flesh.

Thenceforth, he was preoccupied with underpinnings.

A tripper of metal-detectors and wielder of his own. He had a top-shelf model, long as two sabers and heavier. Summer of his twentieth year, this wand went crazy in his own backyard. First exhumed was a pair of antique scissors. A corrosive like rust—but darker—froze the action. Big as veterinary shears, they couldn't be pried asunder. Winston limped over to the clapboard house and laid them on the porch planks. There was no longer anyone inside to tell him what story this was. Mother had passed. Never a father.

"What's down there?" he wondered aloud.

He trudged back for more, his lurching gait like a ball and chain manacled to his ankle. Shirtless and pale, he bore into the red earth like a mite, shoveling on and on into split raw palms. Six deep, the shovel hit upon a metal tube, long and curved with an ovate throat: a scabbard vacant, but nevertheless full of wonder. Winston toiled on, inspired, and next excised a white bone, ambiguous. Then tatters of cloth. Other relics. Soon the shovel was insufficient for what lay beneath.

"More firepower," he told himself.

The backhoe was a Komatsu, yellow as a Tonka truck. It rented by the hour for half what he earned per. The front-end loader scooped out troughs of earth for sifting, and Winston could work it well. Slowly the carcass of history accrued on the front porch: the shears, scabbard, a broken saber, a belt buckle, fabric scraps, the frame of a six-shooter, more shards of bone. Then, finally, he uncovered a ribcage and two white bulbs of empty skull—imbedded fragments exhumed as if from an opened scar.

The porch became his autopsy table. Under the naked bulb heroes were assembled. Soldiers arranged out of excavated miscellany. Empty cranium atop scraps of uniform, armament hung low from no hips. Skeletons construed of artifact, fleshed of imagination. Cavalrymen.

Last-standers before the onslaught of Sherman. *Relations.* Sons come to defend home and hearth from scorched policy, or so imagined. Winston reconstructed them gutless on the planks.

Twilight gathered and he hobbled back into the thirty-foot-wide bowl, ravenous, with him the metal detector. Below his feet lay the bygone scrap heap of history, soon to be resurrected. So prophesized the device, quickening his heart over treasure-rich soil. Surgical metal tripped it, his own. He did not know then that he dug for his own architecture.

The backhoe and he descended like tunnel drillers, earthmoving deep into the night. They pushed on and on, past six feet, past prudence, and found nothing. And then farther. Deeper. Dredging the russet soil in profound swaths, heedless. Winston wanted more than scant slag. He wanted the joinery between.

He found nothing and went to bed by the moon's last wane. As he slept, disinterred brethren bivouacked in his cranium, beguiling him. Fire-ingestive and bellicose, with swords aloft. Tomorrow he would unearth the bones of their warhorses, surely. And the clapboard house, once white, weathered silver—he would repaint it bright as the day ancestors died defending it. Least he could do. Its pitched frame the iceberg tip of a war beneath the soil, and thus imbibed of grandeur. For such he yearned.

He woke to a foul stench. Outside, the dug bowl brimmed with sewage. In the dark, the bulldozer had ruptured a pipe, precipitating the slow accumulation of black sludge beneath starlight. He walked over to the septic tank and tapped. Hollow. One thousand gallons bled dry. Winston turned to look upon the backyard pond he'd fashioned.

"Shit," he said.

A shape floated atop the septage. Winston fished it out

with a freshwater rod. It was a bird. Dead. Drowned in a lungful of feces and urine, thinking only of rest. And not just any winged migrant, but a swan. Trumpeter or Tundra he didn't know. Neither anymore. A swan stained black. Divorced forever from its mate. They were monogamous, Winston knew that much. He knew the pain of rupture too. He brought it over to the house and hosed it down, but the feathers would never be white, the stain too deep.

Twenty years old, Winston clutched the polluted bird to his chest, tight. The bone-structure was more delicate than that of his hand, and hollow. Filled not of marrow or blood or steel, but air. Light enough for flight. Perhaps the truest creature to arc the sky, and its death, his doing. He, club-footed and clumsy, had drilled for the world's framework, eager for stature and stainless girding, and struck only this.

He slogged to the other side of the yard, the soles of his warped feet carving half moons into the soil. There, far from cesspool and leech field, he dug a proper grave, double wide, and in it reburied the soldier pair, or what there was: articles of metallurgy and ivory. He did his best to lay the remnants properly, shears included.

Into the chest cavity of one skeleton he placed the despoiled swan. Razor-bobbed ribs clutched the creature like a heart transplanted. This seemed good to Winston. The sullied creature fit cozy in the man's ribcage, and was protected. A museum may pay for such plunder, but Winston believed himself the better curator. Now he knew what ground he stood.

He shoveled broken earth back over the grave, and it was done. But there was nothing to be done about the pond. Not soon. The backhoe had drained funds to nil. So in the migratory season Winston kept vigil, anchoring himself in a lawn chair for days, his back to the shore. In his hands a 12-gauge shotgun, birdshot extracted from the shells. When the imperial V passed overhead, white as glory, he defended them, firing warning shots, blanks, like an antiaircraft gunner if warring men could be dissuaded so easily.

But swans, they heeded, and no more fell victim to the mire.

SIN-EATERS

They told him the day he turned thirteen. That was the age they'd chosen, in some long ago. It didn't make for a very good birthday. Not in the ordinary sense, at least. Because there was only one gift, if you could call it that.

Few would.

Afterwards, Gilead walked out into the full glare of the winter sun. The trees were bare, and black, their upper branches rimed with a silver glint of frost. He sucked the cold air deep into him, until it burned. Then exhaled slowly, visibly, watching his breath curl away like smoke.

So strange. To be thirteen, a boy one day and this the next. This new thing. Not what you thought you were. Something more, something less. He looked at his hands. The palms were white, with pink creases at the folds. He closed them, opened them. He looked at the sky. A distant spiral of carrion birds, black-flecked against the white sky. A mile off. Two. He lowered his head and started walking toward them.

He could feel the others, shadowing him through the woods. A wide wedge of them. Quiet, quiet. Stepping when he stepped, stopping when he stopped. They had to make sure of course. That this boy had it in him. That he could be one of them.

He followed a path, dark-trod through the snow. Most of it new-fallen, unmarked, wind-piled against the naked trees. But this path, it had been walked before him. The black earth muddled with the snow, boot-printed, a path like spilled ink zigzagging through the trees. The prints, they only pointed in one direction.

Could he do it?

The question burned in his mind.

He'd better.

The wind came up out of the north, a cold blast of it skirling through the trees. He looked up. Saw the naked branches clattering high above him, antlers of crazed beasts fighting for dominance, rule.

He swallowed. Looked at his boots. They kept stepping, as if of their own accord. Something driving them. He could feel the swell of it at his back, like a tide. He wanted to stop. Tried to. Thought: *stop*. But nothing happened. His boots kept stepping.

The trees broke, a great plain of snow shone before him. On it, they waited for him. Furred riders on smoking horses. Ten of them, bearded, with assault rifles slung across their backs. The hunting party. Between them the butcher station, the bloody draw of high-circling ravens. And, before this, the man.

In Town, you never questioned what you were eating. It was meat. Loin or round, flank or shoulder. Often ground, always deboned. You never thought, never questioned.

The man was kneeling in the snow. He was not old, though his face was. Dark circles, sunken cheeks. *Hunger.* But his eyes were piercing and clear, like an owl's. He was not afraid.

There was not enough game, they'd told him. To feed

them all. There had been in the beginning, in the years just following the Eruption, but a decade of nearly ceaseless winter had thinned the stocks. The domestics had all died out. Cattle and chickens, pigs and goats. Little to feed them.

But outlanders, they had plenty of those.

The man was in his longjohns. His hair was wild and knotted. A necklace of boar tusks hung under his throat. He was barefoot. His possessions lay piled in a box several feet away. Boots and coat, backpack, groundcloth, a rudimentary bow. These things would be redistributed in Town.

They handed Gilead the rifle. An M-14, a round already chambered. It was heavy in his hands, ceremonial. All wood and steel. Nothing like the carbines he'd used on the range.

He could feel the eyes upon him. He shouldered the rifle.

Only a few were chosen. Those who were thought to have the requisite character. Who could bear the truth. Guard it. Better not for the entire population to know. No one knew what that might do to their society. Their Town. So it had been decided: only the smallest circle would know. Those who had to.

The hunters.

Or, among themselves: sin-eaters.

Those who knew, so no one else would.

Gilead breathed in, slow. Exhaled, slow. He tried to aim. He tried to keep the barrel from shaking.

In the distance, movement. At the treeline. A bark, high-pitched. A dog. Now more of them. They moved in and among the trees, of a color, like a single gray beast. More barks and whines.

The lead hunter—Vichy— shifted in his saddle.

"He was running himself a pack of dogs," he said. "We tried to get them too, couldn't get close enough." He leaned and spat. "Don't mind them."

Gilead nodded. He looked back at the man. Tears had begun streaming down his cheeks. His face glistened. But he didn't beg, didn't make a sound. He rose taller on his knees, and listened a last time to the howling of his dogs.

Gilead aimed for the man's heart. He closed his eyes. He pulled the trigger.

That night, a feast. In the great hall. In his honor. There was the potato vodka the men drank from pewter shot glasses, neat. Clear fire. There was a stew of turnips, radishes, beets, cabbage. Crops that could subsist in this climate, in the Town's cold frames and cloches. And there was meat.

He sat at the long bench now, with the other hunters. All the Town was there. The girls smiled differently at him, even the older ones. Something wicked in their eyes, in what they offered him. A promise. Everyone knew that the hunters ate the best.

There were many hands on his back, his shoulders, and many glasses of the clear stuff. Many mouthfuls of the meaty stew, and a place at the table set especially for him.

Before the night was over, he stumbled out of the great hall, to the latrine. The torches that lit his path had gone liquid on him, double-forked tongues of flame. He knelt and retched into the mess pit. Retched and retched again. The hunters stood in the doorway, laughing. Telling him it happened to everybody.

They thought it was the vodka.

There were two kinds of sin-eaters. There were the quiet ones. Those who did their job as if they were laying brick, hoeing a garden. No drama. Nothing in their eyes. Perhaps a sad hang in the look of their faces, like old priests. They never forgot. They simply stowed it away somewhere, in the deep of them, where it affected them slowly, inexorably.

And then there were the others. The ones who enjoyed it. Who wore the big cavalry mustaches, the leather riding spats, and always had a new killing device. A blood-grooved lance, a smoothbore pistol loaded with shot. Their cheeks would be red-flushed after the kill, their eyes lit with something. *Desire.* They were always the best hunters.

Vichy was leader. He was one of the old ones, the sad ones. But there was no mutiny among the men. It was no easy thing to swallow, this thing they did. To break down, metabolize into something you could live with. One handled it how he could.

All of them were brave.

In the outlands, where they rode, there was no law. And they were not the only ones who were armed. Plenty of others had stockpiled in the years before the Eruption. In cellars and attics, underground bunkers. Something felt in the blood perhaps, the psychic nearing of an edge. Now there were roving bands of them, hungry. Desperate. Some of them fully devolved. Strange perversions of men, with tattooed faces and necklaces of dried organs. Tongues, ears, worse. So little had survived the snow of ash, months long, and the years of winter that followed. Before long, nothing to eat.

Gilead kept the M-14. It was so heavy. They said it would make him strong. He rode a painted pony, Camo, because she was gray and white. Truly a good combination in the wintering lands they rode. He killed others. Most would have done him the same. They were dragged back to the outland camp on skied travoises, for butchering. The women who cooked in Town prepared only the vegetables. The hunters handled the meat. In the early days, people asked and were told it was wild boar. Something few had eaten prior to the Eruption. After a time, they quit asking.

When the hunters were lucky, they got something else. A doe, a boar. A raccoon or family of squirrels.

They weren't lucky often.

It was said that, in the days before, there was so much meat that people had been fat. Gilead couldn't hardly believe it.

Autumn, not that it mattered. The seasons hardly changed. They were riding a ridge that overlooked a small mountain valley. The trees on the ridge were dead, blighted. Some beetle that had flourished in this new world. It was spooky to Gilead. You could feel their death. So strange for something to die and stay standing. Just hollowed out, rotted, groaning in the wind.

In the meadow below, a broken-down cabin. The roof half-caved, the walls all twisted, the windows rhombic under a burden of unending snow. They had been here before. People—*outlanders*—liked to hide in it. A welcome shelter after so many days in the open.

Vichy raised his binoculars. Focused them. Squinted a long moment into the lenses.

He sucked his teeth, shook his head.

"Not today."

He started to turn away.

"Wait!" said one of the others. It was Niles, his face flushed brightly. "Gimme the 'nocs, I think I saw something."

Vichy handed them over.

"Yeah," said Niles. "Yeah, I got a breather."

They put together a raiding party. Three men. The rest would cover them from the high ground of the ridge. Gilead, with the long-range power of his M-14, and his age, was normally selected for the cover team.

"Gilead," said Vichy. "You're going."

He swallowed, nodded. Dismounted. Checked his rifle, unsnapped the catch for his knife. Niles would lead them, Gilead in the rear.

They started down the hill. It was steep. He slipped twice on rocks, unseen underneath the snow, but didn't fall. He wasn't afraid, not really. He could feel the guns behind him, above him. He could feel them watching over him.

Niles had this big pistol, nickel-plated. His pinky kept coming off the grip, too excited to stay in place. Gilead could hear him breathing.

They made it to the flat land. They toiled toward the cabin, their boots stoving dark hollows in the snow. They passed an old hay feeder, half-submerged, the crossbars hack-sawed here or there for steers with stuck horns. The unpainted rings were red-rusted, the paint bubbled outward from the cuts.

Gilead trudged on. Feeling safe, safe, safe—and then he didn't. It was one step, like a gust of wind, and he knew something was wrong. They were ten yards from the cabin, maybe less. The feeling built up in him. Should he say something? He couldn't.

Could he?

Then he heard the shot. The first one. The man in front of him, Miller, crumpled. He didn't scream, just fell into himself.

Dead.

That quick.

Then other shots, the snow springing around him like something come alive. He started running. Nowhere to go, no hope but the cabin.

He ran into Niles, who wasn't running. Who was standing straight-backed, looking for the shooter. Gilead tripped and fell. He looked up at Niles. The man looked down at him, his mouth twisted beneath his mustache.

"Pussy," he said.

Just then his heart exploded, blasted into a red stain on the snow. Gilead was already up and running, the cabin door hanging slightly ajar. He hit it at full speed, fell crashing into the cabin's interior. Something caught him on the sharp corner of his hip as he fell. He rolled and came up standing in a dark room. He could see nothing, blinded by the snowy whiteness of a moment before.

"Get down," she said.

"What?"

"Down!"

He dropped to his haunches. Felt the shot sing over him, terminate in the far wall with a bang.

Now more shots, other rifles. From behind him. The hunting party, fighting back.

"They won't get him," she said.

He saw her first in silhouette, a big crash of hair on narrow shoulders. And then she began to emerge out of the darkness. Her pale skin, her green eyes. She was sitting on the bed, a coat pulled up over her bare chest. Her feet were sticking out. The soles were pale and smooth, clean. He'd never seen that.

"You heard of bin Laden?" she said.

"What?"

"Osama bin Laden."

He was on his hands and knees. He'd dropped his rifle outside.

"Terrorist from before," he said. "I heard of him."

"Daddy," she said. "Daddy was one of them that got him."

Gilead looked up at her.

"Shit," he said.

More shots in the distance. It was a big gun, maybe a .308 like his. The shots were cold, consistent. He could almost hear the screams of the hunting party.

"He going to kill me?"

"Probably," she said. "We know what you do. The lot of you."

"What we have to," said Gilead.

She cocked her head. "Don't we all?"

And then she began telling him what he had to do if he wanted to live.

He would never forget what happened next. What she revealed beneath the covers. What she'd been hiding. A baby, cradled, wide-eyed and quiet despite the violence outdoors. She'd been nursing him. He had blue eyes, round and big in his face, and skin the color of milk.

Gilead had never seen one. Procreation was strictly prohibited in Town. They just didn't have the resources. The young ones, like him, born in the time before, were allowed. But new births, no. Naturally there were accidents, and these were buried in a plot with the other dead. Inside the Town walls, of course, where scavengers couldn't reach them.

The little one looked at him. Not curious, really. Just waiting, as if the nature of this man would soon be revealed. His mother pulled a walky-talky from somewhere beneath the covers. Gilead had seen the devices before, with the floppy antennae. Vichy had one, for emergency communications with Town. But they never used it. The batteries were too scarce.

She worked a small crank on the side, holding the baby in her other arm. She held it to her ear, heard static, then began to key the transmit button in some kind of precise pattern. It took only a few seconds, and she was done.

"You can go," she said. "Just remember: you don't do as agreed..." She made her hand into a gun and pointed it at him. "Zap," she said.

He swallowed and walked out the door.

The shots had died off. He saw the men on the ridge, crouching behind trees and dead horses. It was a long walk, and he felt like he was going to be shot every second of it. He retrieved his rifle. It was lying next to Niles. The man's eyes were open, staring dumbly into the white and featureless sky.

Camo hadn't been shot. She was watching him as he crawled over the crest of the ridge. Many of the others hadn't been so lucky. But none of the other men had been hit.

"The fuck is down there?" said Tway. He was one of the younger hunters, ambitious and mean.

Gilead looked at him, the others.

"Nothing," he said.

"Bullshit," said Tway. "Somebody was protecting whoever's down there. Whoever or whatever."

Gilead leaned and spat, a discolored clot in the snow.

"Nothing, I said. You wanna go down there and have a look yourself?"

Tway and the others, they looked at him, the cabin, the corpses staining the snow. The silence was eerie, just a hint of wind sighing through the trees.

No, no one wanted to have a look.

That night, he couldn't quit thinking of the little one. That big head, that little body. So much like a little man. It made sense, that being what he was. But the eyes. So open and round. Not squinting like everyone else's, like they didn't want to fully see the world that lay before them. He'd seen eyes like that somewhere before. That clear, that blue. Where? Then he remembered, and he tried not to think about it.

He was glad for the midnight bell. He crept out of his room through the window. He lived in the building with the other hunters, like a clubhouse. He couldn't have them hearing him on this errand.

In the distance, thunder. That was lucky. It would cover him. The streets were deserted, but he kept to the shadows. He was glad to be out of his room. He'd started to thinking of that first kill—the blue-eyed man—and the ones after. Sometimes it got into his head like that, like a fever, and he couldn't get it out. He thought it must be normal, because he'd always thought of himself as normal. But it didn't feel like it. It felt like something else.

The lights were out in the infirmary. There was a big room in the front, where they housed the patients. He crept around back. That door was locked. But he knew the room where they kept the meds. The window was dark. It wasn't barred. Meds were valuable, of course. They couldn't be reproduced. But no one stole them, not in Town. Theft meant exile, and nobody risked that.

He found a broken chunk of brick. He took out the shirt he'd brought just for this. He wrapped one in the other, and waited for the thunder. He threw the brick through the window. Then listened: nothing. He reached through, careful of the remaining shards, and undid the latch. He lifted the window and crawled through.

The silence was haunting. He could almost hear the echo of daytime life. Perhaps just the pulse of blood in his own ears. He found the right cabinet, opened the satchel he'd brought. He was breathing hard now. He thought he heard something in the hall. Had he? He hurried. He lit matches to see the labels in the dark. This one, that one. She'd been very specific.

Something in the hall again, a scrape. Like someone trying to move quietly in the dark. The last one, it had to be in here somewhere. He couldn't find it. He had to get out. He could hardly breathe. He swept the remainings into his satchel, the bottles he hadn't checked.

A scrape again. He ran for the window. He was afraid

now, truly, like he hadn't been in a long time. So afraid he forgot his shirt.

He should have seen it coming, the storm. He knew, but he didn't think. They'd rode out at dawn, as was their custom, and he'd brought up the rear of the column, as he always did. They rode in file through the woods, old to young, and sometimes he wondered if that was his future there before him. His evolution. They rode lower in the saddle, the older they were. The sadder. At least the ones he cared for. The ones like him.

He'd already felt it inside him. The way it haunted him. The nameless hurt, like a poison in the blood. Like your body rejecting it. Your mind. It was something you couldn't get out.

But now, but now he had this. This hope in the satchel. Because he wasn't only going to give them what they needed for the baby. He had been to the edge of it, to exile. The night before he had. And now he was going to choose it. He was going to be part of them. They would want him. He knew the woods, he was good with a gun. And he wouldn't have to be this anymore. This thing. He would be free.

When the trail forked at the old snowed-under schoolbus, where they could choose to hunt north or south, the column went south. Gilead, he went north. It would take them some time to notice. Too long. He would be away. They would backtrack, but it was starting to snow now. His tracks would be gone. He would have simply disappeared. No one would mourn. His parents were gone, of course, long gone. Maybe one or two of the girls, the ones who made eyes at him and came to his room at night. But he didn't want them. He wanted the clear eyes, the unbroken heart. He wanted to be like the snow. That's why it was so pretty. It was pure and it was clean. Not like him.

He was a mile down the north road, toward the cabin, when he realized his mistake. The snow was falling heavier now. When he stopped the horse he could hear the whisper of it in the trees, on the road. It was telling him something. That it wasn't going to stop.

But he kept riding. The world beginning to close down on him. He might have turned back. But he knew he couldn't. He could feel it. Something he'd felt before. That he was being followed. Shadowed. He looked over his shoulder, twice, expecting dark shapes in his wake. In a world gone white, ghosts must be the color of shadow. But there was nothing. Just the snow coming down slantwise and slow. He thought it must be his nerves.

So he kept on.

"We'll make it," he told Camo. "Don't worry."

It got worse. The snow coming down in curtains now, ledges. He was so happy for the blighted wood. It meant they weren't lost. He rode to the edge of the ridge and looked down into the valley of the cabin. It was nearly obscured in the wind and snow, just a dark hulk—a shadow—in the bottomland. One second you could see it, the next you couldn't.

He rubbed Camo's neck.

"We made it," he told her.

Just then the world erupted. Shots and screams, bulb-like flashes in the snow-laden air. *Ambush*. The battle swirling behind them, around them, violent shapes rearing suddenly out of the miasma. Tway, staggering, holding his gut. A red patch flowering under his hand. In his other, a pistol. He looked up at Gilead.

"Betrayed," he said.

He raised the pistol.

Camo wickered and reared. Gilead was thrown from the saddle, crashing softly, strangely, into the down-like layer of newfall. Then he was up and scrambling, falling, rolling down the ridge into the valley.

They'd followed him. They'd known. He didn't know how. But he could hear the Navy man's big gun booming through them. Killing them.

He surged through the snow, knee-deep, toward where the cabin should be. Swinging his arms this way, that way, battling the snow every step. The world blown sideways now, all white. The shots and screams muffled strangely, distorted, whipped in and around him, beside him one moment and faraway the next.

In all this, in all this there was still one good thing he could do. He had the satchel clutched close to his chest.

For him, he thought. For him.

He broke through the cabin door. It came down with him, and then he was up again, in the dark room of a day before. She was there, in the bed, the baby swaddled heavily now against the cold.

"I'm sorry," he told her. "I'm sorry. I didn't know."

He held out the satchel. She started to reach for it, but froze, her head cocked, her hand shaking in midair.

"No," she said. "Oh no."

And then he heard them. *Dogs.* So many of them, their barks and yelps all come together like a single guttural thing, a giant beast roaring through the woods untamed. Unkillable. You could hear the blood-shrieks of the dying. The men, the horses.

"Take him," she said.

He looked down. She was holding out the baby.

"What?"

"The roof," she said. "It's the only place."

He was holding the baby before he knew it.

"What about you?" he said.

"The meds were never for him," she said.

And that's when he saw it: her leg. She'd pulled the covers back, and he almost couldn't look. The teeth-marks were clear, on the inside of her thigh, crowned in discolored bruises and oozing darkly, blackly, and stretching outward from the bite the infection, the sick cloud of it under her skin, green-rotted and foul. He could smell it, it was so strong.

There was a shotgun too, a wingshooting double-barrel sawn short for close-in work. He realized she'd had it on him every moment.

"Go," she said. "You have to go."

He did. He went out of the door and around the house to where there was an old barrel that had once held whiskey or water. He held the baby close, as he had the satchel, and climbed first onto the barrel and then onto the roof, kicking the barrel over as he did. He wasn't sure if the old rafters would hold, but they did. Seconds later the dogs appeared out of the snow, a dark mass of them like a tide. They were of a color, as he remembered them, ash gray, but the pack had grown, multiplied, so that they flooded the valley. They went through the door and he heard the first barrel, the second.

She didn't scream.

And then they wanted the roof. They crowded the walls, leaping and snapping. A sea of them, red-mouthed, their wolf-teeth bared. They had been pets once, he'd been told. These killers. Sedate on their leashes and in their crates. Heeling when told, shaking hands for kisses and treats.

The cabin shook with their fury, shuddered, a hundredfold moiling of beasts throwing themselves into its walls, rib-boned and desperate. How long could the rotted old timbers hold?

He held the baby close. It was so warm, and it didn't cry. He could feel something emanating from it, not just warmth but something else. A power, like something atomic. He could feel it go into him. Into his blood. Deeper. Down into the meat of him. The core. The eyes looked up at him, and he looked back, clear-eyed. Full of wonder.

He was still looking when the first shot from the big .308 came streaking out of a tree on the ridge and brought down a dog on the edge of the pack. Immediately the others descended upon it, tearing it limb from limb, and by then another had been picked off, this one farther from the cabin. Then another, another, and before long the dogs were far out into the valley, devouring themselves in a red hysteria, like a great wound in the snow.

Gilead came down off of the roof and began making the long walk to the trees out of which he'd come. He clutched the baby close against his chest, and he could feel it pulsing, pulsing, as if it were his own heart.

RIVER OF FIRE

The roar of outboards broke the marshland hush, throttles to the stops. The "No Wake" sign hung slightly crooked from a barnacled post in the marina, the red letters smeared by years of salt water but still readable. Hunkered over a flat tire in his shop by the river, Hector Francis could identify the boat without looking: *MVP*, a tournament kingfish boat helmed by the big league pitcher who lived two miles up the coast. Built on a 36-foot offshore hull, the boat was propelled by dual straight-six engines, 300 horsepower apiece, the throaty howl of them unmistakable in the otherwise still afternoon. The boat boomed full song through the No Wake Zone without slowing, whipping whitecaps from tidal blackwater.

Nobody bats an eye, thought Hector, shaking his shock of red hair. His own 13.5-foot sea kayak could cut silently through the water, sleek as a minnow in aquamarine blue. *To each his own*—but the breakage bothered him. The ballplayer, however, had become the pride of Hampton Island. His very presence elevated the price of real estate and lured tourists to the riverine resort that supported the income of most residents. So people kept their mouths shut, Hector included.

He'd had but one encounter with him. The pitcher had twins, girls, and at the beginning of summer, they had come to the shop to rent bicycles. They were eight or ten years old, Hector estimated, and quite cute—much cuter than their progenitor. Despite his seven-figure contract, the big-leaguer had balked at the posted price of rentals. Called them criminal. Hector, who'd inherited the bicycle shop two years prior, adjusted prices according to inflation, no higher. To insinuate otherwise was just short of fighting words. Not that Hector himself was a fighting man—far from it.

As the wail diminished into the distance, destined for open water, Hector stuck his tire tool back between the rim and rubber of the bicycle he was repairing, one of his rentals. A one-man operation, his establishment rented bikes to tourists from the big resort that fronted the river. His were big pondering bikes of lugged steel; they hummed quietly down island bike paths, greased to run without creak or clatter.

Hector liked that, the quiet. Thin as a reed, waif-like, with skin the translucent hue of a milk carton, he'd always found the world of senses intrusive. Sunlight cut through him like shallow water and loud noise addled him right to the bone, scattering his thoughts like a school of baitfish. Internal combustion was the worst. So he preferred human-powered locomotion. That seemed only logical for an island not ten miles long, not five miles wide.

Lucky for him, most of the tourists thought the same.

He heard the bell jingle and hastened back to the storefront, assuming position behind the register. In walked a family of five. They looked around at the bikes, mouths agape.

"This the yacht club?" asked the father.

Hector got that question a lot.

"No sir," he told them, "it's right around back."

"Oh," said the man, "thank you." He and his family fumbled out the door backwards.

The yacht club inhabiting the other half of the building shared the same square footage as the bike shop: not much. It was not a yacht club at all in the traditional sense, but an office that offered fishing trips and nature rides to guests of the resort. No fancy dinners or cigar rooms, though it did sell knit shirts with an embroidered shield of arms.

Hector went back to the shop and began prying the tire off the wheel with a pair of steel-girded levers. Inside, the tube was fully flat. He pulled it free, reinflated, and then began to brush the long black tube along the sensitive skin of his cheek, slowly, until he felt the tiny whisper of leaking air. He saw by the slit-shape of the puncture that it was only a pinch, the tire itself not compromised. He patched the tube, placed it back inside the knobbed rubber, and kneaded the tire back onto the rim by hand.

Afterwards, Hector attempted to bolt the wheel right back onto the front forks but failed, putting the wheel onto the truing stand instead, his head hung low in resignation. It was a habit he couldn't shake. Spinning the rim, he peered along the black tread for the slightest quiver of warping. This one wobbled faintly, a millimeter's breadth. The imperfection was hardly enough for the most discriminating French racer to notice, let alone an overweight Virginian riding off the previous night's shrimp and grits. But Hector saw it.

Turning slightly on his stool, he opened a drawer behind him, no need to look, and got out his spoke wrench. If nothing else, his two hundred rental bikes gave the truest ride of any in the county, every one of their alloy wheels made straight through long hours of balancing each and every 10-gauge spoke to unquivering perfection. When the bell rung to announce the next set of customers, Hector did not even hear them, sunk as he was in the nature of his work.

The next morning was Saturday, the week's mad rush of weekenders. Hector filled out hard paper tickets for each set of riders, the same analog system perfected three decades prior. Then he doled out the bikes one by one, sizing inseams to frame geometries, fine-tuning by seat height adjustment. Test rides were taken; extension of leg at nadir of pedal stroke analyzed. Hector had once hired local high schoolers to assist him, boys three-fourths his age, but they had no regard for fit or trim. So it was just him, his exposed flesh lathered with sunblock, his hands strong upon adjustment levers and hand tools. The two o'clock lull gave him time for lunch, a brown bag of sandwich, apple, and cookie he'd made himself. He made six on Sundays, saving one day for lunch out. The phone rang. On the other end was Alfred, king drunkard of the yacht fleet.

"Hector, you ain't even gonna believe this."

"Believe what?"

"I been around the water a long time, son, and I never seen the likes of this."

"Of what?"

"You ain't even...I swear."

Hector scratched his head. "Well," he said, "give her a try, why don't you?"

"Damn—I got customers. Just go out to the dock and see for yourself. Over the edge near the fish trough. Gotta go." He hung up.

Hector held the dead phone away from himself a moment and examined it, pursing his lips. The he shrugged and grabbed his keys from their hook under the counter.

A white gate, barred prison-like, guarded entry to the marina, but it was wide open at this hour. Not far beyond it hovered the tin box of the fish trough, irrigated by a garden hose. A clear sluice of water ran glistening down the center groove, channeled for clearage of guts and blood, and cascaded over the edge in a clean arc to the shallows. Hector stuck his hands in his old khakis and peered over the edge, ten feet down. There in the shallows, in hardly three feet of water, lay a manatee floating belly up, her ponderous side fins keeping her mouth positioned right under the falling stream of hosewater, her mouth slurping open and closed, drinking.

"Sweet Jesus."

Sea cows, they were often called, and the Conquistadors had thought them mermaids. Hector had never comprehended that belief, big and bloated as they were. Never had he been so close to one. She was more than ten feet long and must have weighed close to a thousand pounds. Her wide-set eyes were black and friendly, her dog-like snout bristly and jowled, her massive body haloed in concentric rings of surface water. No spout like that of a whale or dolphin, Hector watched her nostrils flare wide, breathing in the familiar fashion of a land mammal.

Not really pretty enough for envy, he saw, and not quick enough for meanness, she floated there in the tidals like God's very own idea of innocence being fed, the garden hose giving suck as if mankind made pap of his ingenuity. Hector felt as if he could stand there on those wooden planks and watch her for the rest of his life, his world silent but for the low murmur of running water and the hush of their common breath.

But then the manatee rolled slightly to keep the flow, and in doing so revealed a pink worm of scar—fresh—that curled snake-like around her body. Then she rolled still more fully, letting the cold current run down her back, and Hector could hardly keep down a hot bubble in his stomach. The wound was so fat, the girth of a boa constrictor at least, and it raked her humped back as but one of countless scars, chalk-white cravats of churned flesh. Tears stung in his ducts, trembling in saline fury.

Hector looked out at the river, a faint rippling surface that belied what universe thrived beneath. Organisms of alien design, jellied and luminous of tentacle, jetted through the depths by strange modes of propulsion. The jelled grotesqueries might be built for eternal darkness, but not the manatee, a sea mammal evolved of prehistoric land mammoths with four legs. Like him, she saw in color, and Hector worried how she could find her way in the brackish obscurity of marsh water, the world of sight but a foot-length of green-brown submersion chock-full of tidal minutiae, weedgrass, and six-hole soda can binders of white plastic. Hector had not been victim to the squeeze of sweet-panged talons for more than a decade, but he was now. His heart pounded like a bloodied fist, his throat constricted to the tiniest jet of air, and he was gripped by an insane urge to vault the railing into the blackwater beside her.

Just then he heard the squeal of children's voices. The pitcher's twin daughters, prepped and dressed identically in pink sundresses, came barreling toward the dock, skirts billowing like blown roses. Alfred and their mother followed behind. The pitch of their happy shrieks made him cringe, shrink, and Hector was drowned suddenly in the righteous flood of his own possession. Backing away to give them right-of-way, he bumped into the fish trough. His hand, steadying him, groped the flat handle of the fillet knife left there for charter captains. With no thought of why, he gripped the hardwood, either side screwed to a long hone of slightly curved steel. Behind him it gleamed like a scimitar, though his body blocked sight of it. The children would never have noticed anyway, enthralled as they were by the swelling proximity of the sea mammal.

The two of them leaned far over the water between slats of deckwood, chattering in voices strange to him. Hector thought he might be able to decipher the shapes of their words should his mind allow it, but he did not listen. Instead he watched their splayed fingers grope toward the animal. He was not going to use the knife—never—but the blade lent him the full swell of guardianship—enough to share his bounty.

Alfred and the girls' mother—the pitcher's wife—arrived.

"There she is, Mrs. Slocum," said Alfred, pointing as if she did not readily notice the phantasm of marine biology floating right beneath them.

Then Alfred walked over to Hector and punched his shoulder.

"Did I tell you, Hector, or did I tell you?"

Hector kept both hands behind him, clasped there as if in courtesy.

"You told me," he said.

"Damn right I did."

The mother, a lean forty-year-old of veined fitness, glared at them.

"Excuse me, ma'am," said Alfred, looking sheepishly toward the children. He sidled closer to Hector, retreating from her. "I been around this river a long time," he said, his voice low and guttural, "and I never seen one so far inland. You think she's lost?"

"God, I hope not," said Hector, and said it with such urgency that Alfred raised his eyebrows a little.

Across from them, the mother had moved to the railing, standing tall and stately between her twin daughters.

"That French they're speaking?" Alfred asked her, nodding toward the children.

"Yes," she said, not looking at them, and Hector could hear the accent in her voice. Then she leaned over the railing, tightening her pants across her legs.

Alfred nudged him with an elbow, the camaraderie of their sex, but Hector was paying no attention. Instead, he followed the children's eyes to where the manatee was breaking from the jet of freshwater to paddle for the river. Ahead of her, the barnacled post of the "No Wake" sign arrowed out of the shallows, her tortured rotundity swimming toward it dumbly, fatalistically, and Hector with no way to stop her. As the bottom deepened beneath her, she submerged. Just a black wake betrayed what swam beneath, no foam. Hector squinted far down the river bends, upstream and down, hunting for the faint sight or sound of a coming boat. Even with Alfred so near him, he could not let go the knife, gripping harder still to think what violence he might do the careless boater who came round the bend, no regard for what soft bodies swam beneath the twin or triple harrowing of steel-driven vortices.

Tiny palms still clutched for the submerging mammal, wanting her back. Hector saw them coveting her not for salvation's sake, but to own her, a great aquatic pet to live in their swimming pool like a fish in an aquarium. He wanted to draw his weapon and leap between them, his back to the manatee, his blade flashing to defend her in the slanted light of afternoon. He would protect her from being sold off to a Floridian waterpark when they tired of her. But he could not blame them, not really, because of the desires that had lodged in his own gut within the last ten minutes. To feed her raw fish he bought from the market, to nourish her on hosewater, to landlock her in an above-ground pool where no rules could be broken but his own—he wanted all this for himself.

Hector put down the knife. Gently, to make no sound.

Just then the flat drone of a boat broke across the water. Hector squinted to see the white bow of an incoming vessel come round the bend. As it neared, he identified the howl of those twin outboards long before the family members could. When they did see who it was, the three of them, tall mother between twin girls, began to wave and jump with enthusiasm enough to catch his attention. Hector, meanwhile, hunted the surface worriedly, hunting for the red blossom where flesh and steel might intersect.

The pitcher kept the throttles pinned right up to the "No Wake" sign. Then he noticed his family. He yanked off the power and looped 180 degrees, sliding the big boat into an open slip with a jolt. Behind, a near perfect circle of white-churned wake floated atop the water, no blood that Hector could see. Relieved, he watched the girls clamor down the ramp between boats, their mother trailing behind, the both of them talking at the same time, chattering in the same strange language of smooth syllables, pointing frantically toward the river.

The pitcher, a tall man whose gangling limbs gave snap and power to his fastballs, put one hand atop his ball cap and held out his opposite palm like a traffic policeman. His daughters did not halt; their mother looked at him and shrugged. Though the ballplayer wore wrap-around sunglasses with polarized lenses, his brow could be seen crinkled in confusion, as though the velocity of language was too much for him.

Though Hector himself could not understand a single word of the language, he made his own translation of the children's meaning. He reckoned they were asking their father to try and catch the mammal lumbering somewhere beneath them. Catch her for a pet. That was what *he* would have asked, anyway, were he a child in their position.

Hector looked past them at the kingfish boat's gleaming heraldry of razor hooks and brass reels, spools of high-tensile fishing line and saltwater rods of every length. Tools to pull fishes from the depths, quick and quivering, they hung along the gunwales like the implements of a medieval armory. The pitcher had hung them unevenly, in no order of robustness or length, and the stout tapers of graphite—so many of them—seemed of a gauge too heavy. Meanwhile the outboards continued to chug, emitting plumes of smoke that curled across the water, blue and purple, while twin flowers of stainless steel churned the rear of the boat into a bubbling well of whitewater.

Hector thought vaguely of the knife again, but with the sleek white vessel floating before him, the slow burn of another idea began to illumine the dark corners of his mind. But it was only the smallest spark, just a fragment of a vision really, and much afflicted by the clamor of engines and voices. He shut it out, standing alongside Alfred in pained spectatorship. Soon thereafter, the ballplayer and his wife got into an argument. Above the short blonde heads their hot words raced back and forth, these in English. Something about money. Alfred tugged Hector's sleeve and gestured toward shore. To listen would be indecorous.

Hector consented, looking a last long time at the otherwise glassy water, the pit of his stomach like a tank of cold water. Then he started back up the ramp, following Alfred. When he got back to the shop, three separate sets of customers were hovering outside his door, arms crossed, waiting for service. He was rolling bikes into a neat echelon for them when the roar of gunned outboards shook the steel frames on their kickstands. The anger spoken through those big engines needed no translation. Even as the ballplayer's wife and daughters came back up the ramp, exiting the marina, the hulls of moored boats jostled violently behind them.

Dusk came late at this latitude in summer, but well into darkness a yellow slat of light could be seen below the shop-house door. Hector huddled over his work table in a long session of truing rims, eating his next day's lunch for dinner. For in that silver silence of spinning hoops, spinning like pulleys or gears of a frictionless world, he had no thought of broken zones or the wreckage of flesh. To make each wheel roll true, he tightened and retightened along the whole circumference, working until the radial skeleton achieved perfect alignment.

The floorspace of the shop was as small as a walk-in closet, but Hector had arranged the tools of his trade with the ergonomic forethought of a jetfighter cockpit. Each tool had its place, reachable without thought or look. This pleased him. He had been born early into the world, of course. Before he was ready. And, by death, left alone at an early age. With hardly double-digit years beneath his belt, he went to work for the man who had built this shop, the last scion of a family of tradesmen and smiths. No son of his own, he gave the shop to Hector in his will. One day, the old man, who had lived through two heart attacks and one round of chemotherapy, swerved one of his rental bikes to miss a tree-frog crossing the sidewalk. He swerved into the road, and a one-ton landscaping truck did the rest.

From then on, the shop was Hector's. The income was plenty enough for him. Nothing exorbitant, but he was not a man who envisioned his life as a rising monument, ever accruing stories upon a tapered base, hungry to skyscrape. No, he felt a sharper alignment with the quiet cycle of these discs, trying to keep their rhythm true atop a world of jagged pavement and broken glass, potholes and steep curbs. Long ago, he had learned that this took well-observed maintenance, late hours, and—sometimes—a table-vice and mallet.

  Hector came early to work the next morning, sliding the rubber-coated lock-cables from the long rows of bicycles and wiping the dew from their seats. As soon as the marina opened, he strolled as far out as the fishing trough, ostensibly to take in the view, and truly to turn on the hose. In an age of waste, no one would notice the faint leak of freshwater.

She came early that day, the manatee. And many a day after that. In the early morning hours, before the day's profitable rush of bicyclists, she came. Or later, in the last light of dusk, when the water was glassy and thick. Like him, the sea cow must not have liked the clamor of fishing tours, the tromp of boardwalkers. And always he kept the hose running for her.

Then, exactly one week after Hector's first sighting of her, she disappeared. Hector stood looking into the shallows, watching blue crabs side-straddle across the bottom where she used to float. He felt out of balance, his head heavy as a leaden wrecking ball, his neck hardly enough to keep it upright. His hands clutched the old split wood, steadying him on the impalement of countless splinters.

Two nights later, a photograph near the back pages of the local newspaper depicted the beached carcass of a manatee, or what was left of it. The article stated that marine biologists from the Department of Natural Resources found the cause of death to be trauma inflicted by the propellers of a passing boat. The biologists concluded that the manatee, which was female, had been surfacing for air when the strike occurred, and that the boat was traveling at a speed of no less than thirty knots. The author of the article then offered an explanation of the species' endangered status and advised caution to local watersports enthusiasts.

As he stared at the grainy photograph of mutilation, black-inked against a glaring strip of sand, Hector Francis felt the violent spin and wrack of unbalanced orbit. Like a rock-bent rim throwing flaps of tread across the highway, his head reeled, and sparks, like rage, tore through the dark of his skull. In no world of his could such deep intrusions go uncorrected. The vast and fluent cycles of the world, of tidal surge and outgo, of deposition and erosion, of death and birth—these the most eloquent of mechanisms—had to be kept operable, or the gears and ratios of tide and time would grind into disharmony, and red gore would trail in their wake. The cycles were greased to run on a thin film of blood, but man had taken to making the world in his image, a linear path of logic with ambition for closure, finality, and no forethought of the engines of history bled to a dry husk, the terrible screech of that halt.

Hector crumpled the paper into a ball of dusty ink. He needed to recalibrate his world, which tottered, and he knew beyond doubt which screws to turn, and with what torque. But he did not want that, not now. So he went out to the driveway, got in his truck, and drove out to the shop. There he bent over his worktable for another session of truing, hoping to allay his afflictions in another long midnight of corrected shapes. In quiet fury he worked, working past hunger and exhaustion, but minute adjustments escaped him. The nerves of his hands and arms longed for fast-twitch contraction, thwarting finesse. In the morning, a slew of mangled wheels were piled in the corner, broken ellipses that would not satisfy.

Two nights later, dusk was darkening the riverfront as Hector closed up for the night. He had received two complaints that day of bikes with wheels warped enough to drag upon their brake shoes, but still he could not seem to fix them. All he could do was think of that broken body on the beach, an image that wouldn't be dislodged, and his blood burned and burned like its chemistry had been knocked out of whack.

As he slid the cable-locks through the neat rows of bikes, the twin outboards of *MVP* sounded from far up the river. Hearing that, he inhaled as if before a long dive and went inside. There he selected three items from the shop miscellany at his disposal: a length of plastic tubing, a permanent marker, and an old rag dipped in oil.

Meanwhile, the pitcher hurled the boat into an empty slip like a first inning heater, ignoring the "No Wake" sign like usual. When he and his wife staggered past the shop, talking loud of next year's playoffs on their way to a nice dinner at the resort, Hector gave them the polite wave of his station. The twin girls, dressed in white evening wear, followed behind them unspeaking. They returned his wave as their parents did not.

The resort was an old-fashioned one, the clubhouse itself a great white structure with dormer windows, black roof, and a wraparound front porch half-obscured from the marina by a line of gnarled oaks. After the family ascended the front steps and disappeared inside, Hector cut the lights and locked up for the night.

At this hour of late twilight, nobody was in the employee parking lot. The shifts of the resort staff did not match his own. But he was given a specified parking space, number 113, and there his old Ford half-ton sat parked. The hull of his sea kayak glowed blue in the bed of the truck, as always. And as always, a two-blade carbon paddle and kayak-specific vest lay alongside. Black, with cross-strapped buckles and the hard sheath of an inverted river knife, the vest had the look of something a commando would wear. In the rear, a large pocket was stitched for a hydration bladder. Hector extracted the bladder, a clear sac not unlike the medicine drips of hospital rooms, and detached the top. Likewise, he unscrewed the gas cap of his truck and threaded the length of shop tubing down into the tank's interior. Once it struck the bottom, he put his mouth over the open end and sucked, watching for the shadowy trace of liquid to come down the tube. When it did, he transferred the tube from his mouth to the mouth of the bladder, siphoning into it a liter of fossil fuel for ulterior use.

It was completely dark now and he searched the lot again for company.

Seeing no movement, he slipped off his sneakers, stuffed his socks into them, and put them inside the toolbox. Then he slipped on a pair of winter paddling gloves, full-fingered, and slung his arms into his vest, angling the bladder's drinking tube away from his mouth to prevent an inadvertent suck of 87 octane. He hauled his kayak on one shoulder to a trail that led down to the riverbank.

At water's edge, he hovered a moment. The river was black glass under sparse stars and a sliver of moon. The mud was cool between his toes. There was no sound but cicada and the casual lap of waves. Hector slid the bow into the current, feeling buoyancy take the weight from his arms, and wiggled his lower body into the shallow hull. He dispensed with the spray-skirt, opting instead for quickness of egress. Then he pushed off. Soon he was far out into the river, paddling smoothly, flicking one blade flat while feathering the other to a whistle.

Ahead the marina floated on half-hidden barrels of blue plastic, airtight. It was dead at this hour. One weak floodlight illumined the walkways, but every one of the several boats bobbed darkly, inside and out. At the last far slip floated *MVP*, the upward rake of her white bow sitting higher than the others. Hector slid by the "No Wake" sign with hardly a ripple. He moored his kayak to one of the stainless cleats on the outside of the offshore boat and slipped over the side. Crawling on all-fours, he untied the infinity-shaped mooring lines and pushed off, letting the big boat drift free with the current. As it floated toward the center of the river, he took out the bladder of fuel and began hosing down the deck with unleaded gasoline. After that, he opened the fuel tanks.

Hector could hardly breathe now, such were the fumes. They smelled of quick death, curling deep down into his glands and heart. Satisfied that all was set, Hector stood upright for a moment on the deck. The boat rocked gently beneath him, but his eyes leveled upon the twin outboards, unmoved, and he was pleased to find balance amid the waves. The white of the hull shone like ice in the darkness, very pretty. It had to be. He could not exact flesh for flesh, so the handsomest of boats, sunken, would have to remit what washed ashore.

He slipped back into the kayak and paddled to what seemed a safe distance. Knowing his throw had better be a good one, good as any late inning fastball, he balled the rag and got out his butane survival lighter. In one movement, he cocked his arm, lit the rag, and hurled the igniting fireball along a trajectory that arched high into the night, hovered there an agonizing moment, and dropped like a comet between the gunwales.

Scrawls of flame zigzagged across the decks, greedy for fuel, and then erupted skyward, a bright harlotry of pointed tongues. Hector dug the carbon deep beneath the surface, distancing himself in short bursts from the expanding heat. He kept just ahead of it, head low and hunched, paddling with balls of acid for shoulders. Then the tanks blew. Ten trucks' worth of gasoline. Hector turned and saw, with wicked joy, the outboards dynamited skyward in bright jets of flame, twinned in wreckage. Then, a moment later, a white tongue of ignited gas shot low across the water, shooting straight through a blizzard of broken fiberglass, shooting straight for him.

He capsized the kayak and went under, kicking for the bottom. Around him, superheated fragments of hull hissed into the depths. He opened his eyes into the black sting and saw, above him, a blazing firmament. An oil slick had spread across the surface, ignited, and now he was trapped beneath a lake of manmade fire. His own. There, hovering weightless beneath the surface, he was forced to make a decision left mainly to young boys at a game of morbid hypotheticals. Between one mode of death and another. Between burned alive and drowning.

The oxygen slacked in his brain. Hector had warped the night to chaos, blasted bright fissures into its darkness, and given no thought to spilled toxins or the spread of fire on water. He looked around for his manatee, looking for help, but she was nowhere in the strange dark glow of burning water. Nor could she be. And if she were, not even she could have stayed under until the flames died, the flames he'd ignited for her, and that seemed to make ruin of all his calibrations. The water started to warm around him, the depths beckoned. Hector thought of the placental darkness from which he'd been thrust too soon. Part of him wanted to stay here until he too evolved, reborn into a creature with fins and tail, needing no land to live.

But as darkness enveloped him and his circle of vision collapsed, a cold jet of despair shot through him, giving vision to his legacy: a front page story in the local paper, by the author of the manatee's obituary, telling of a disgruntled ball fan whose plan of sabotage backfired—a story false, giving nothing to the blameless suckle of beloved dead, no spark, and he with no way to true it. His heart quickened then and he looked up to see a black fragment of broken sky. High stars wavered through the vent of darkness, undulant pixels in the heat, and though Hector could not tell whether they were stars of the night sky or stars his own, he kicked toward them, kicking for the dark wreckage of all his reckonings to save him, the black fragments of a blasted hull.

On the bank stood the pitcher, his wife, his twins. All of

them in white. They, like their neighbors, had left dinner cooling to see what glowed orange beyond the ballroom windows. The pitcher's boat was unrecognizable; he knew it only by the empty slip. Furious, he started to tear off his ball cap to stomp on, but succeeded only in mussing his neatly combed hair. Other spectators noticed the fit. Whispers began to circulate through the crowd.

"It's the Slocum boat," they said. "Who would do such a thing?"

"Probably a woman," said one man.

"Or a *Marlins* fan," said another, joking.

Profanities quaked in the pitcher's throat, wanting release.

But each to each, his daughters grabbed a hand, averting an outburst. They spoke in English now, knowing he understood it better.

"Papa," one of them said, "it was a bad boat for the manatees anyway."

They had thrust this line hard on him the last week. He'd been standing staunch though, taking side with his boat. But they, these miniatures of full-grown women, did not back down easily.

"Nonsense," he told them, but wondered. He wondered too at the river of fire, how awful it was, and a sudden dread gripped him.

He squeezed his daughters' hands.

"Maybe," he told them, "we can get us a different boat next time. One of those airboats. Flat bottom, no propellers. Would that be better?"

"Yes, Papa!" exclaimed the two of them, his twins, squeezing his hands in their own. The gripping warmth of those tiny hands, the warmth that bound them, would hold him to all his promises. They reached out and took their mother's hands, closing the circle of them into a single shape against the night. His family smiled then, even for the whispers, their faces like jack-o-lanterns in the floating blaze.

The pitcher managed to smile too, but still he wondered what madness must lurk beyond them, in those black depths beyond the flames. And somewhere in the deep of him, where he kept things never to surface, he remembered the sickening bump of impact. He'd been trying to keep that truth down, hidden, but what burned before him peeled back darkness like a torch. And with the blaze hot on his face, on his smile, he wondered whether all the madness was within him or without.

WHOREHOUSE PIANO

She played whorehouse piano, bawdy and loud, on a 1901 stand-up with bubbling paint, red-coated over black, under a ceiling brown-stained with water spots. She, Lucy, had straight-chopped bangs, black, like she'd done them herself with kitchen shears, and cheek bones so high and firm they made dark razors of her eyes, just a wink of vision in them.

No one listened to the piano, the songs so well-keyed to damage and abandon that no one could hear them, like the way you forgot your own breathing. She played soundtrack to their unfolding dramas, ass-groping and well drinks and *let's go upstairs, honey.* They staggered this way and that in the dimness of smoke and glass, in this nowhere place where they could be something other than the bad-inked tattoos that swathed them like bruises, too muddy to decipher.

Tables sat in broken ellipses, chairs off-kilter with a shorted leg, the whole barroom an assemblage of wreckage picked up from the floor again and again, daily during the closed hours of daylight by skilled barkeeps who set them teetering for those scant hours before darkness fell.

That was Lucy's favorite time. She came from the barrage of daylight, the mean Louisiana sun, into dank darkness, the spotted ceiling arching high overhead, like spoiled heavens. She crossed the barroom floor on flagstones of light thrown down from the high windows, her stepping stones laid out in fours that matched the windowpanes, the cruciform darkness that divided them.

She did not go into the darkened corners. She stepped from light into light, careful to avoid the tenuous erection of tables and chairs, and then she stepped the six inches onto her stage, that dizzying height, and swept her dress underneath her to sit on her stool, the toes of her red high heels set daintily on the pedals, her red-painted fingers and scar-nicked knuckles crackling in preparation, like a prizefighter's before they put the gloves on.

The keys rang more crisply in that quiet time before nightfall, the light fading, the congregation of wrecked furniture sitting broken-backed and hulk-like before her. She did not sing then, singing only when other voices could drown her own. She hummed, her once-cut throat glistening whitely in scar.

Later the working girls. They came clear-heeled with fancy purses slung underneath their armpits, the newest fashions bright-spangled and fringed. Lucy had been one of them, of course. In her teens. Driven from home to here, hardly different, forced to conduct and indulge all orifice, all pleasure. Some of the men liked to see blood, hers, but she had teeth, nails, knucks, and did the thing she'd learned long ago to do, at home: fight.

Now she played the piano, no whoring, her voicebox coarsened with grit, her voice itself a hard and perfect rasp for the songs she played.

Her brother came looking for her on a black night in July, a guitar case slung over his shoulder.

"Papa's dying," he said.

Lucy had already played thirteen songs about death that night, each more tragic than this. She told him to tell the family he couldn't find her. She told him he didn't know nothing about daddies and their little girls.

The man who'd done her throat was Patterson Goode, known everywhere as Whoreson for his temperament, or how it used to be. He did underwater work for the Gulf rigs, globe-helmeted with breathing hoses and undersea torches. He stopped the black clouds that pooled underneath the water, the leakage of cracked pipes. He welded fissures and busted girding. He kept the rich men in Houston getting richer, the black gold sucked twenty-four-seven from the earth's crust.

Whoreson carried an eight-inch fixed-blade in his boot and loved Lucy more than anything, his cheek white-raked by her nails, his shoulder moon-stamped by her teeth. He listened to her songs now and called her a pianist, the only one. He no longer drank or frequented whores and had to buy other people drinks to earn his seat. He would have killed her Daddy in a heartbeat, had she asked him to. Still he said she should go see him on his deathbed.

Lucy started playing a wordless tune left-handed and lit a cigarette with her right. Then she looked at Whoreson.

"He can die without me," she said.

"I'll go with you," said Whoreson. "We can take my truck. I got three days till next shift."

He looked pleadingly at her, needing, as always, whatever redemption she'd give him. Her nearest eye cut him up and down, steel-specked.

"Tonight," she said.

They drove all night into bayou darkness, low-hung moss and the scarce reflection of blackwater amid the mangroves.

Highway signs reared before them, bleary and wayward-tilted. Red-flattened carcasses of small mammals littered the road. Whoreson crossed himself when he saw them, reborn. Her hand retreated when he tried to hold it. They never touched, not since the night he slit her throat.

They stopped at a truckstop outside town, too early to wake her family. They drank burnt coffee from styrofoam cups under the yellow florescence. Lucy saw little black things huddled at the corners of the hanging lights, insects dead in brainless awe of Louisiana Power & Light.

At dawn, they took the backroad to the little house where she'd grown up, the sky-blue paint weathered green, vines clawing upward on all sides, the whole house moldering slowly back into the fecund swampland on which it sat.

Lucy told Whoreson to stay in the truck. She pushed her door open on its rusty hinges and shut it and approached the rip-screened porch, moths with wide-eyed wings clinging to what screen there was.

Her mother and brother came to the door in pajamas, her mother heavy-footed with gnarled toes. Lucy had perfect feet, sleek and shapely, like her father's.

They led her through dark rooms that smelled the same as they always had, that made her feel the passing of time all at once. How much she'd done, seen, sang, and everything here the same. The brown carpet, the yellow linoleum, the faucet bleeding rust into the kitchen sink.

They'd made the sickbed in her old room, her father swaddled in damp sheets, his breathing jagged as glass in his throat.

"Throat cancer," they whispered.

She bent over him, his closed eyes, her piano hands crackling into hard knots of fist. He would die peaceful in this blue room, no one to blame him for anything that had happened here. Lucy wished she could claw down into his innards and pluck the words out of him, the ones she wanted to hear: the *I'm sorry's* and *please forgive me's*. She wanted to see fear in that gaunted face, fear of what might be coming next when you left behind the kind of legacy he did, when you wrecked things in the dark and never turned on the lights.

Her brother and mother stood behind her. Lucy looked at them watching, no knowledge in their faces, not hearing the cacophony erupting inside her skull, like they never had. She reached out to touch her father, a final gesture of some kind, but could not open her fist. She turned and walked out of the house, the screen door banging behind her.

Whoreson saw her coming and leaned over; the shotgun door creaked open. She got inside and told him to drive home. He nodded.

On the drive back, they drove right into the rising sun. It rose white and clean over the cripple-armed trees, the twisted trunks and swamp. Whoreson squinted into the new day, his face unravaged in light, the busted pilings of his teeth white where the sun struck them.

Lucy looked at him.

"If you hadn't of almost killed me, you never would of been saved. You'd be at your old ways, whiskey-drunk, cutting whores. You ever think of that?"

He nodded slowly. "Don't seem real fair, huh?"

Lucy looked out her window and nodded. Then she shook a cigarette from her pack and lit it, cracked her window a half-turn of the crank, and blew the smoke outside.

Whoreson looked at her.

"You did save me though. I believe that. You're like a angel to me."

"Like hell I am," said Lucy.

But a sudden urge ran at odds to her words. She wished she were already back at the whorehouse tonight, at her piano amid the night's wreckage, playing a song for this one man who would listen. Who wanted to. She touched the scar at her throat with her thumb, and then she put both hands on the dashboard, the cigarette slanted sideways from her mouth, and started to thump a tune on the sun-warmed vinyl, a low voice of song rising from her cut throat.

Whoreson didn't look at her for fear she'd stop.

HOME GUARD

He doesn't look so tough for a hero, if that's what he is. He's way too short first of all, like five foot nothing. Looks like he's still in high school, even though he's a couple years older than me, and I'm about to be a sophomore. At State. Before now, the last I'd heard of him was when he did Mallory Dawson in the back seat of his black Mustang convertible. We were freshmen, Mallory and me both. She was my sweetheart then, though she didn't know it. She was starry-eyed for older guys, guys like David Doogan laying in wait to steal her virginity. Son of a bitch. He became my arch-nemesis then, though he didn't know it.

I hadn't seen Doogan in about five years when I saw him at the bar last weekend. He looked the same as always, except for two things. First, he had these veins running all down his forearms. Looked like a map of the Mississippi Delta I once saw. He isn't so big, as I was saying, but those sons of bitches gave me pause. Other thing was his haircut: buzzed Marine Corps style. All that had changed him. He might've looked downright dangerous if it wasn't for his posture, all slumped-like. Backbone hunched, shoulders pushed forward—not what you'd expect from a Marine.

Anyways, when I got there Doogan was talking to this

guy Bear. His Dad being a urologist, Bear is loaded but tries to act like a redneck. Drives a street truck, wears camo, has a pit bull on a chain leash named Attila. That truck of his—it has a goddamn aerodynamic wing on the back. If that's not in bad taste, I don't know what is.

Bear was just towering over Doogan, talking up close to ear, and Doogan was just standing there with a draft beer in a plastic cup, nodding his head. Right then, any old bitterness I was harboring about his exploits with Mallory evaporated. I don't why.

When I walked up to them, Bear wheeled on me and said, "Wyatt! Doogan's been shot!"

I gave Doogan a thorough perusal. He didn't look shot to me.

"Shot?" I asked. "Where at?"

"Son of a bitch was a sniper, Wyatt."

"In Iraq?"

Bear nodded. "Killing towelheads," he said, "and camels."

I looked at Doogan and gave him a substantial head nod. I've got two such nods. One's where my chin goes up. That's the one I give when I reckon I could kick a guy's ass. The second one is a downward nod of the head. That's the one I gave Doogan, you can be sure. And I'll give it to anybody who's taken a bullet. I even gave it to Eddie Lovett one time, who shot his own self in the shoulder hopping a fence with a shotgun in tow. Dumbass. Even still, I gave him the downward nod. I don't know what it is to be shot, but it's something.

"You okay?" I asked him.

Doogan nodded. That was when I noticed he had himself an acne breakout, just a couple of red petals on either side his nose. Besides that, his face was pretty white for a boy who'd been in the desert for so long. He started to say something, but Bear's big head swung between us.

"Got shot right here," said Bear, jabbing a fat finger just above my pelvic bone. Last damn place I wanted the son of a bitch sticking me.

"Hit his flak jacket first."

I looked over at Doogan, his mouth just hovering somewhere between open and closed. Not much to read in it.

Bear went on. "Only went in yea far, or thereabout." He made a two inch space between thumb and forefinger.

I leaned over toward Doogan's ear and asked what round it was.

"AK-47," he told me.

"7.62 by 39 millimeter," Bear said. "Full-metal jacket."

"Where'd it happen?" I asked.

Doogan looked at me and I saw his mouth shape a word, but it got swept away in all the gabble and bottle-clink. Bear leaned over to translate for me.

"Fallujah," he said. "Goddamn bloodbath."

I'd seen some pictures of Fallujah in *Newsweek*. All the buildings were the same color and that was the color of sand.

"Shit," I said.

Doogan leaned toward me and said some more, but the din in there blew his sentences all to shit. Luckily I could pretty much string together the story on my own: rooftop, convoy, waiting, sunset, nothing, spotter, extraction, helicopter, stood, shot, dead.

As he talked I nodded my head real gravely, like I was stone sober. At the same time I pictured him all decked out in desert camo and black webbing, grenades and canteens and flares and pistols and all. Just this little guy and his spotter and a big .308 sniper rifle with the heavy barrel trained on a corner in the road. Waiting for some bad guys to come round the bend and them not coming and the sky getting dark and cold and no helo to pick them up.

Seemed to me he was telling this story like he was telling a whole other one. Can't really explain it, but I tell you, he wasn't talking like no Rambo. Looked more like Mr. Youngblood, my old Bible teacher. Full of holy dread and all that.

Me, I was just matching up his words with the pictures I'd seen. From what I could gather, they'd got stuck up there on that building way behind enemy lines. Chopper wouldn't come, LZ too hot. So it got dark and them all alone. Finally a Blackhawk arrived all decked in green lights and turning the dust off the rooftop in big tendrils, and when they stood up to clip into the ropes somebody with an AK-47 opened up on them. Full-auto. His spotter didn't make it and Doogan took that one in the gut.

This whole time Bear was hopping up and down on his toes, too tickled. Finally it burst out: "Show us the scar!"

Doogan strained a fake smile. I could tell it was fake because it showed too many teeth for a boy who wasn't telling a teeth-showing type of story. Then he peered down at his shoes. Bear, he looked down there, mouth agape, then looked up again.

"Show us the scar!"

He was getting squirmy now, Doogan was. Fidgeting a lot for a boy trained as an expert in sitting still for maybe days at a time. Pissing in his own pants if he has to. Now looking sheepish as hell, like he spilled something he shouldn't have.

"Show us the scar!"

Believe you me, he didn't want to show that thing at all. I nudged Bear in the side. Thought he'd get the message to lay off. But Bear just looked at me with these beads of sweat trembling across his lip, and then he turned back to Doogan.

"Wyatt wants a peek too! Come on, son!"

He was looking everywhere but at us. Doogan, I mean.

Me, I was just looking at Bear and calling him a jackass in my head, feeling like the world's greatest asshole just by association. But then, just as I was about to apologize to Doogan, I saw him raise up his shirt.

It was not like any scar I'd ever seen. I expected a pale circle where the scarred skin was shinier than the rest, but this was a wound: black, blue, purple, yellow. And real big. Size of a donut at least. Just looking pissed and mean and new. I was pretty grossed out, to be honest with you. Shit was pretty horrible to look at. Made me feel my own kidneys swimming down there in my guts.

Next thing I know Bear's got him in this big hug. Big bear hug you got to be big and hairy as Bear to give. Hell, almost made me want one myself—not to be gay or nothing. How it made Doogan feel I don't know. Before I could gauge him, a group of local girls came by. Doogan greeted some of them, but me and Bear just kept to ourselves, talking like we had shit to attend to. Important matters. You know the routine.

Bear put his hand on my shoulder.

"You know that big sniper rifle, the Barrett .50 cal?"

"Fine weapon," I said, nodding. From what I'd seen on TV, that thing is just about as tall as me. Same bullets that shot down Zeroes and Messerschmitts.

"Damn right," said Bear. "You know they use that honker to kill cars and airplanes and generators and such. Shell is yea long." He spread his thumb and forefinger as far apart as they went.

To all this I was nodding a lot.

"Just put one right in the motor," said Bear. "Kill it. Anyways, I was asking Doogan if he'd shot the Barrett and he said one time indeed they had him hiding out in this culvert with it. There was this field in front of him and nothing was supposed to cross it. Those were his orders.

Nothing crosses. No cars, trucks, wagons, camels, nothing. Nothing that moved. You got me?"

"I hear you."

"Anyhow, he just sat there for near on two days and nothing. Said not a thing come to pass. Then finally there comes this big-ass truck. Said *kubz* or *hubz* or some Arabic shit on the side. Whatever, it was the Arab word for bread. Big old bread truck. White. Well, he puts one in the engine block. Stops the son of a bitch cold."

"Yeah?"

"*Oh yeah*. Anyways, driver gets out thinking he's just broke down. Goes around back and gets out a big plastic shelf of bread and starts lugging it across the field."

"Then what?"

"Well, what you think? His orders was nothing crosses. That includes bakers, don't it?"

"Is that what he said?"

"Nah, he didn't really say. I had to *infer*."

"Shit."

"What you think that does to a man?"

"Shit," I said again, shaking my head. I wasn't sure what more to say. My mind seemed stuck like the engine of that bread truck. Pistons not turning over.

"Can you imagine the nightmares?" Bear asked me.

I couldn't. I just looked over there at where Doogan was standing amongst those girls. They were just jabbering on every side of him, talking amongst themselves. He standing there like the new kid at school. Awkward-like. Acne making it look like he was blushing, and maybe he was. Hands in pockets and shoulders all scrunched. Like he was having to keep all his blood and heat from spilling out.

He'd been a real good skateboarder once, I recalled. Back when he'd done Mallory. Didn't look like much of one now. Wouldn't look like much of anything if it weren't for those veins swelled along his forearms. I reckoned those spoke more than anything else about him. I had the feeling he'd tried to tell me something but I missed it. I followed those veins down to where they twisted into his pockets like ropes. I tried to see the hand that had pulled the trigger on that baker and God knows what else. But I couldn't. His hands were hid too deep.

He looked my way and I gave him the deep nod again, trying to tell him I understood it all. What it was to be a killer of men. But I don't think he saw me. Either that or he knew me for what I was. I can't say I wasn't jealous of him.

COVERED BRIDGE

Baker stepped rock to rock, downward, his bare toes gnarled for traction on the slick-tilted planes of river rock. He watched for gaps that could swallow a leg, angles that could break an ankle. His palms were sweaty, a loose-handled satchel gripped in one hand.

Below him the river hissed and whorled, eddied drunkenly at elbowed corners of boulder-rock, then jetted whitely ahead, rapid-foamed, and Baker knew the real danger lay in the black-shooting hydraulics that ran beneath the surface, that could knock you from standing and hurl you crammed under a hunk of rock old as the world, leave you there amid the bone-jammed carcasses of deer and dogs and children gone missing.

That would never be him, he told himself. His thirteen-year-old body was muscled and lean this summer, hand-made himself in the high school weightroom, looking to play tailback come sophomore year. A match for near anything short of the varsity defensive line. They still outweighed him by nearly a hundred pounds a man. But his time would come, he told himself.

He reached a big flat-topped hunk of rock, big as a Volkswagen, perfect for sunbathing if the climb down wasn't so tough. There were many other paths to the river, easier ones, which his scantily-clad peers used on weekends to find sun-bright planes to lie out over the water, to drink beers and frolic and tan.

But days like today Baker preferred the shade of the covered bridge. The covered bridge had been there as long as he could remember, red-roofed, past it a ten house community of working families who'd built it. That was Moss land up there, or had been—Moss his mother's family. All the houses up there had been of one side that family or the other, blood or marriage. But now those houses were gone, leveled, the families paid out well to move somewhere else, to the edge of Lake Lure mostly, making room for the luxury homes planned to go in their place, thirty homes where there used to be ten.

On the high side of the land, where the earth went shallow before the rising crust of rock, was the graveyard where his mother was buried, the dirt churned black over her grave.

Baker crossed the big flat rock and climbed down the other side, into the shadowed cool of the bridge. He sat on a chair-shaped rock, his feet dangling in the black rush of water, and opened the satchel he carried with him.

Flowers. Day lilies mostly, red-orange as a girl's lips, and azaleas too, these his mother's. Dead now but not yet the seeds she'd sown. Not yet. His father wanted them cut, gone. He didn't care how or where. Baker had scythed them down this morning with his pocketknife, pulling handfuls of them taut like you would a throat before cutting. They came loose, light as air, flowering from his hand, petals tickling his skin like fingertips.

They'd buried his mother in a casket, full-bodied, instead of cremating her to ash, as she'd wished. He didn't know how it all came about, probably something to do with his father's family, Presbyterians all. They did not believe in degrading the body, as though they'd never seen the rotting carcasses of livestock mangled in barbed fencing, as though that degradation didn't transpire in a person's coffin.

Baker palmed a handful of flowers from the satchel, their brightness undiminished by the shade. He examined the petals, so tender. The day lilies you could eat. His father used to make day lily fritters, batter-fried golden. Baker lowered his upturned palm toward the rush of water, the bottom stones long smoothed by hydraulic action, no edges to them, serene despite the torrents that ripped over them year on year.

A clamor downstream stilled his hand. He looked up. Bare-backed locals were standing up on their rocks, dumping coolers of silver beer cans into the river, throwing away ziplock baggies of weed and pills. Uniformed men were descending the weekend trails, shuffle-footed, hands steadying their sidearms, black sunglasses down-tilted to watch their steps.

The cops never bothered anyone out here, no one local, not until now. Baker heard steps above him, on the slatted pine of the bridge, then on rock.

"You, boy, get up here."

Baker looked up and squinted at a black shape thinned against the overwhelming power of the sun. He nodded and started back the way he'd come.

"Bring that bag with you. That's the reason you're coming up here."

Baker nodded and stooped down to pick up the satchel and climbed four-limbed up the rocky creekside, his dry skin making good friction against the crags, the bag draped over his shoulder.

He stood finally before the policeman, a young man with a starched shirt and shaved head.

"Let's see the bag," he said.

Baker handed it to him, his heart beating like he'd done something wrong.

The police officer swiped open the satchel with a rigid hand, cocked his head to see inside the black well of cloth.

"What you got in here?"

Baker swallowed. "Flowers, sir."

The man's brow crinkled.

"Flowers?"

He shook the bag over a flat-topped stone, just a few of the orange and pink flowerheads falling upturned like bright propellers onto the rock. Pink and purple, some red. The lilies orange.

"These some kind of funky flowers, edible?"

"No, sir. Those is just day lilies, and those others azaleas, my mother's."

"Your mother's?"

"Yes, sir."

The man squinted at him, suspicious. "What's a boy like you doing with all them flowers?"

Baker stiffened. "Nothing," he said, too quick.

The policeman nodded his head like he was beginning to understand. "Son, ain't nothing illegal about being a—"

"They're just pretty is all," said Baker.

The man looked down at the bladed petals, like flowers from rock. He cocked his head from one side to the other. After a moment he exhaled.

"Shit," he said, "I reckon they are."

He handed the bag back to Baker and looked over his shoulder. He was young, his face round and unlined.

"Listen," he said. "You best just get on out of here. There'll only be trouble down here today." He nodded downriver, boys chest-puffed against handcuffs, their girlfriends hip-leaned toward their badged captors, flirting for freedom. "You don't want any trouble, I'd get on."

Baker nodded and squatted down to gather up the loose-strewn flowers before walking back the way he'd come, walking quick and light as he could to salvage his soles against the scorch of the blacktop.

At home he placed the satchel in the garage refrigerator, where they kept beer and soft drinks, placing it in one of the empty vegetable drawers where his father wouldn't notice.

"Where you been?" his father asked, looking up from his paper.

"Down at the river."

"Don't you got a gym regimen to keep up?"

"It's Sunday."

"My day, there weren't no days of rest."

And look where that got you, thought Baker. He looked out the bay window, the glass heat-warped, to the hills rising green-folded from their yard, steep as walls. You could not even see the tops of them from inside the house. You had to be out there, right underneath them, looking straight heavenward like a kid in the front row of a movie theater, a trick of angles keeping you from ever seeing the peak, the summit, only the last ledge of barefaced granite you couldn't ever reach.

"You take care of them flowers?"

"Yes, sir. Buried them. Full-stemmed I did."

"What's that matter?"

Baker shrugged. "Reckon it don't."

"Well, you best just stay away from the river. I hear they're trying to pre-sell half them homes before the bulldozers even get cranked. They don't want no riff-raff hanging round the river, scaring off them buyers from Charlotte, Atlanta."

"Yes, sir."

Come midnight, Baker was huddled underneath the covered bridge, his bedroom window agape some mile distant, the satchel left in the fridge, too risky to wake his father.

Diesel hulks roared and smoked on the far hillside, angular earthmovers with square white eyes. Baker heard more of them traverse the bridge above him, tank treads squeaking like reinforcements. Long drips of oil fell through the slats overhead. Tiny spouts of steam hissed on the cold black water.

Baker was rigid with gooseflesh, his skin alien on him, the fine mist off the running snowmelt so cooling in daytime, so frigid at night, no sun to fight the cold. He'd not expected this, had gone barefoot as always, his black wife-beater worn as camouflage.

A wooden fence was going up around the perimeter of the community, head-high and barbed ornately with gold-tipped spires.

His mother had owned a parcel of land up there, a half acre was all, but green and unbuilt, willed to his father at her death. A short walk through sparse trees to the Moss firepit, the banjo and mandolin and yearn-filled voices of singing kin. He'd always thought he'd live there, but it had been sold alongside all the Moss land—his father's doing.

Baker palmed the hard square-cut piling beside him, the wood damp-dark over the gush of water, like a tide had risen when he wasn't here. He held his hand there, flat-palmed, and felt the fine mist against his knuckles, the wood darkened by invisible flecks of spray. The wood was unsodden by so much whitewater, just as sturdy as the days it stood living from the earth, bark-bound and leafed.

He patted the wood and slid his hand upward, against the grain, asking for splinters. His hand disappeared into the shadowed joinery overhead.

Senior walked down the stairs stiff-jointed, skipping the loose and rickety steps where news of his going might groan into the upper reaches of the house and wake his boy. He snuck a six-pack from the back of the garage fridge and walked out toward his shed, through the yard, weaving between the broken white flagstones, the grass crackly and cool underneath his bare feet.

The tin corrugation of the shed held a strange luster in the darkness, like it lagged behind the rest of the world, still reflecting the last glimmer of dusk.

For most his days he'd been a dynamiter in the rock quarries all around the state. They would send him rappelling down sheer rock walls with his rope, his gear, his explosives. All day he'd drill one-inch holes in the naked exposure of rock, striated century on century, and neatly insert his sticks of TNT, running fuses from the blasting caps to the T-handled detonator on a far ledge. At end of day he'd watch his handiwork blow dust-white towers into the blue sky, eons of granite and shale blasted heavenward, broken, raining down hotly into the carved-out bowl of earth, there to await the trucks, the grinders, the stone-cutters.

That was until his fall, his broken back. The doctors told him he'd been lucky his spinal cord wasn't cut, no paralysis. He walked carefully now, stiff-spined, like something might still slip, some sharp-edged bone fragment of his past cutting his legs from underneath him.

He opened the shed and stepped into the dark. Found the cache of candlestick dynamite hidden in a cardboard box labeled X-MAS LIGHTS. He started descending the path through the woods, three sticks in hand, the six-pack under his arm.

Senior's johnboat floated silently in the middle of the lake, the moon an ovate silver sheen across the surface. It did not touch the quadrant of black water he'd chosen.

He slurped the last sip from a can and set the crushed aluminum in a bucket alongside its companions. He lit a cigarette and inhaled, then touched off a TNT fuse with the ash. It crackled like a sparkler. He tossed the stick over the side, the white spark haloing through the air. It hissed when it struck the surface, sank.

Senior leaned to watch, one forearm shielding half his face. The dynamite had come with sixty second fuses, but he'd cut them down to fifteen, timed to blow like depth charges. In his day he could eye a fuse better than anyone. He'd won many a bet over fuses crackling nakedly against the white rock-dust of the quarries, cutting them by sight alone to burn a given number of seconds.

He waited, watching the white spark descend deeper, deeper. Nearly disappear, the seconds down to one. The white seed exploded ball-shaped from the depths, outburst like a supernova, the lake suddenly electric with power, illuminated, the depths exposed white-lit a single second, the hull hovering suddenly high and weightless, as in air, over a sunken rowboat, tiny from such height, and schools of stunned fish, limbic and unswimming, their scales silver-struck.

Senior sat back in the boat, looked heavenward, blinded. He closed his eyes and imagined the fish rising all around him, white-bellied, their bladders ruptured, specking the black surface in droves. He palmed his way around the bottom of the boat, found the net.

"Trout for breakfast?" asked Baker. "We never eat nothing but fish around here. Don't seem natural."

Senior waved the greasy spatula in his direction.

"Jesus Christ was a fisherman, boy. And I never heard him getting huffy about it."

"Well," said Baker, "seems like we might could stretch for something different every once in awhile, what with all that land money."

Senior set the thick china plate down hard before his

son, the silverware rattling on the table. Flaky pink meat bleeding a yellow pool of butter. Then he set down his own plate, hard too, and took his seat at the head of the table, Baker at his right hand, an empty chair across from him.

"Let's say grace," said Senior.

"Grace," said Baker, picking up his fork.

By nightfall Baker had already crossed the bridge onto the old Moss land. The workers were on dinner break, or maybe changing from dayshift to night. No one was hardly around. He walked up across the construction site and up the far slope to where the headstones shouldered out of the earth in broken formation, his mother's the whitest.

There were no pretties to grace them, no glass vases or new-cut flowers or notes hand-scribbled for the dead to read. He knelt over his mother's grave bare-kneed, the earth still soft and dark, and the ground here felt warmer, safer, like some remainder of warmth and running blood infused the ground. Some spirit. He spread his hands flat to the dirt, soaking what he could through his palms, and then he clenched handfuls of the black dirt in his fists, let go and clenched more, his hands burrowing of their own accord, like animals for warmth or to escape some predator.

"Hey, boy! Get away from there!"

Baker bolted upright, black-handed, his eyes wide. A big man in a hardhat was barreling toward him, his finger pointed in judgment. Baker looked down at himself, his hands, the torn-up earth between his bare feet. He took off running down the slope, heard the man yelling behind him.

"Graverobber!"

Bobcats and backhoes littered the hillside, stacks of wood, and men suddenly everywhere, stepping down from newly arrived trucks, big men with hardhats that gleamed under the halogen worklights flickering to life in the dusk.

Baker felt his velocity build, faster and faster downhill. A workman lurched from behind a yellow digger and Baker dodged him, spinning, running straight again until another man, this one white-chested and tattooed, hunkered low before him, readied. Baker juked left, right, too quick to follow. The man crumpled before him, as if spell-struck, and Baker shot past.

He vaulted a sawhorse table from a higher ledge, the angles right, and landed sure-footed, still running, and felt something whelm up in his lungs, the hot rasp of exertion but something else too, the river nearing, the bridge, his power crescent, too fleet-footed to be caught, and he was almost there when the blindside came, exploding skull to skull from the right, his footing lost, his body wheeling downhill, rag-dolled, toward the river rock.

He woke to a halo of grim faces arched over him, above them the bruise of dusk. The square and hair-grizzled jaws were moving but he heard nothing save the monotone ring inside his skull, like a far-off siren.

He turned from the faces, saw where the river ran sunken through crag-rock only a few steps away, the covered bridge straddling the silent sluice of dark water like a shelter of some kind, red-shingled and shadowed from heavy snows and the mean-boring sun.

The voices started to break through the ringing, but barely, like the low gush of running water. More pleasant the lightning bugs, their bulbs flickering yellow like the tiny lanterns of tiny men, moment-bright and gone.

Baker sat up, his world dizzied, and started to stand. A heavy hand kept his butt to the ground. He could not quite decipher the exact words delivered him, their separate shapes and meanings, but understood their message. That he could not come back here. That his kind was not welcome. No dirty-footed mountain trash, no black-handed graverobbers. No trespassing.

"Moss," he told them. "My mother was a Moss."

No exceptions, they said. No names carried extra weight, especially names they'd never heard of, like Moss.

Arms hooked underneath his armpits and lifted him to his feet, dizzied, no surety in the ground underneath his feet. Hands ushered him toward the open maw of the covered bridge, that once shelter, now like a tunnel bored through the air where none was needed, a one-way path to his past. No future of Moss land, not even a grave.

His feet crossed the slatted pine of the bridge, the river hissing darkly beneath him, the rocks jagged and black and wet. All around was shadow, night come early in the shingled darkness. Ahead the outlet, the squared light of dusk, the old mountain highway whose broken shoulder would lead him back to his father's house.

He crossed the threshold, stood, turned to look back the way he'd come. A lightning bug drifted before him, the vertical body and disc-like wings hovering like a miniature hummingbird, that delicate. The white bulb on the tail ignited, yellow-lit, and Baker reached out and caught the luminous being in the hollow of his cupped palms. He could feel the tickling flutter of tiny wings.

He looked up the darkening slope of the hillside, past the gold-spired fencing and the earth-moving equipment, past the worklamps and helmeted men, to the sparse stand of trees where his mother lay buried. So far-off, and not but one way across, this bridge, and that thwarted by men at the far threshold, their arms crossed, their bodies growing one-dimensional in the falling dark, silhouettes only, dark and unyielding as a wall themselves.

Baker clenched his hands into a double-handed fist, maddened and powerless. He wanted recourse, had none.

No way to tell them this bridge was his past, this land his future. No voice they would hark, no sledge but his brittle knuckles. He unmade his two hands until they made a prayer shape against his chest.

Only later, after hiking most of the way home, the broken-shouldered highway rising crookedly into the dark upper reaches of the mountains before him, did he open his hands from their steepled place against his chest and see the crescent smear in his palms, luminosity burst against the black lines of grave-dirt. A sad sight to behold, sadder still because he could think of no other end to the short dream of holding the world intact.

He kept on walking, calm-hearted despite the ringing in his concussed skull, walking another mile up the mountain hollows to the dark country of his home, his father's house, the glimmering shed where his father kept the Christmas lights hidden from his son—or thought he did.

Come dawn, the blue-ridged highlands grew around the flat mirror of the lake, upthrust, their peaks articulated out of darkness against the rising light. Senior's johnboat chugged across the water in blue puffs of smoke. He pulled up to the warped dock where he stored the boat and tied it to a rusted cleat. He climbed out, another night's catch heavy over his shoulder, and zigzagged down the uneven planking, no sleep to steady him.

He needed to sell off his catch while it was fresh, and the riverfront grills would already be opening, happy to buy fresh fish at a big discount, no questions asked. He trudged toward town. Before sunup there were few police around to ask questions, no heat to turn his catch foul-smelling and unsellable.

All night, his boy's dinnertime bitterness had stung in his mind. Senior had only done like the rest of the family, the Mosses, selling off the land at a good price, and the money he'd stuck in a trust for the boy's future, college or tech school or something. Baker believed he could get a full ride playing football, despite his size, and maybe he could. Still, he needed a way to bridge one future to another, should the first go crooked of its aim. In Senior's experience, only money and firepower made you any kind of real change in the world.

Senior stood on the deck of the river grill, the chairs still stacked on the tables, most his catch sold off to the cook preparing for Sunday brunch. The cook had thrown in a can of cold beer, and Senior popped the ice-crusted top and slurped the contents, the river flowing past in white V's around jagged hunks of rock like the kind he'd blasted once from sheer mountainsides.

He was thinking of that, his past, when a boom exploded in his chest, a blast from upriver. Senior dropped to his knees, his ears ringing, his beer foaming across the deck. No one else in the county had the explosives for that kind of blast.

No one else.

He was still on his knees, his hands gripping the deck railing, his eyes set stinging on the water, watching for debris, for blood, when the flowers came cascading down the dark shoots of water in bright flurries, wheeling and fresh, the petals like frozen outbursts of color. He saw them and knew they were lilies and azaleas cut long-stemmed from his wife's garden, cut by his boy, flourishing the river like some kind of parade, and Senior thought of the short-cut fuses of his dynamite, cut to blow so much quicker than the labels read, and he could think of nothing but his boy, his boy.

He closed his eyes to the blossoming flood, the terrible hemorrhage of beauty in the river, and crumpled fully to the deck, hearing only the river run onward, so jagged-toothed and sweet.

IN THE SEASON OF BLOOD & GOLD

Pale light crept into the black stanchions of pine, the ashen ground, the red center of dying coals. The camped men rose silent and broke the bread of old pillage, hard as stone, between blackened fingers. One of their number looked at his own. Soot and powder, ash and dirt. Neat crescents accrued underneath the nails, trim and black, like he'd tried to dig himself out of a hole in the ground. Or into one.

Some of the others chewed loudly, bread dry in dry mouths. No tins rattled. There was no coffee, not for some days. He wanted always to talk in this quiet of early morning, to speak something into the silence that uncoupled them from the close pallet of slumber. That assembled them into the crooked line of horsemen, no colors among the trees. No badges, no uniforms. He wanted to ask what quietude might linger if they hovered here longer in the mist, did not mount and ride. But they always did.

So he sprang up first. He shoved the last crust down his gullet and kicked old Swinney where his britches failed him, an inordinance of cloven white flesh.

"Goddamn katydid," said Swinney, second-in-command.

"Least I ain't a old ash-shitter."

"You be lucky to get this old, son. Right lucky this day and age."

The boy set his cap on bold.

"Lucky as you?"

Old Swinney hawked and spat a heavy clot of himself into the coals.

"Luckier."

They rode horses of all colors, all bloods. Strays they called them, tongue in cheek. Horses that offered themselves for the good of the country, under no lock and key. The quality of a man's mount was no measure of rank, a measure instead of luck and cunning and sometimes, oftentimes, cruelty.

The boy went to mount his own, a fly-bitten nag with a yellow-blond coat in some places, gray patches of hairless skin in others. She'd been a woman's horse once, most likely. The men had used to joke about this. Then one of their favorites, an informal company jester, was blown right from her back. The mare had stood there unmoved, flicking her ears, biting grass from the trampled soil. No one save the Colonel enjoyed a horse so steady. They left off joking.

The boy stuck one cracked boot into the stirrup, an ill-formed shape clanged from glowing iron by an idiot smithy. Or so the men had told him. They told him many such things, their faces fire-bitten and demonic over the cookfire, the embers circling them like burning flies. The boy believed them all. Never the facts, the names, or the settings. But what they were getting at, this he believed. There was faith in their eyes, so black and silvered—like the move of steel in darkness. He believed in what hands torqued them to speak.

Rays of dawn shot now through the black overhang of trees, spotting the ground with haloes of warped design.

The rest of the men slung themselves into their saddles, a cadre of stiff-jointed grunts, and some of them stepped their horses into the light unawares. The boy saw them go luminous among the black woods, specter-like. Like men elected to sainthood. Faces skull-gone, mouths hidden in the gnarled bush of their beards, showing only their teeth. The equipage of war hung by leather belts, pistols and knives and back-slung scatterguns of all gauges. This hardened miscellany jolted and clanked as their horses tapered into the long irregular file of their occupation.

They rode the forest until the white face of the sun hung right above them and the insects clouded so meanly men soiled their cheeks and foreheads with dirt and ash. The horses flicked the mosquitoes from their rumps with their tails. The skin of man and animal both grew spattered with spots of burst blood. They rode unto the verge of a small green valley of sparse trees. There was a farmhouse down there, a barn. Out of habit they stopped for lunch though there was little to drink and less to eat. They stopped within the cover of the trees so as not to be seen from the valley below.

When the boy dismounted his horse, old Swinney slapped him on the shoulder.

"Welcome to Virginny," said the old man.

"Virginia?" said the boy, his eyes going wide with wonder.

He crept toward the edge of the trees, his face dark amid the shadows. He could feel the older men's eyes upon him, their ears attuned to the snap of stick or shrub. They listened because he made no sound, this boy, the lightest of foot among them. A former horse thief, his skills translated readily to their pursuits. At last he stared down upon the rough-planked barn, the once-white house, the single white pig mired in a sagging pen of mud. He stared down upon Virginia for a long time, a stranger unto this country.

When he returned the men were tightening the holsters they wore and sighting their rifles and sliding their knives back and forth in their sheaths, back and forth, making sure no catches might slow the draw. At this juncture the boy was possessed of a French dueling pistol of uncommon caliber. He mounted up and pulled the heavy j-shaped weapon from his belt and thumbed the hammer back. The filigreed metal of the action spun and clicked into place over the rich wood frame scarred by countless run-ins with his belt buckle, tree branches, roots where he'd dropped the thing practicing his pistoleer skills.

Swinney stood below him.

"You got any bullets left for that thing, boy?"

The boy held the pistol toward him butt-first.

"She's a firecracker," he warned, smiling.

When the older man reached for the pistol the boy dropped it sideways from his hand and hooked it upside down by the trigger guard and spun the gun upon its axis and caught it by the backstrap, the trigger fingered, the barrel at Swinney's chest, the older man's eyes wide with fright.

"Let them sons of bitches learn the hard way," said the boy.

In fact he did not have any bullets. He was out.

Swinney's eyes narrowed and he shook his head.

"What you need is a good ass-whooping, boy. Not them parlor tricks."

The boy spun the gun twice and stuck it in his belt.

"Now don't you go getting jealous on me, Swinney."

The older man made a derisive gesture and waddled down the line.

The provenance of the pistol was known—one of a pair from the vast arms collection of an officer they'd kidnapped from his bed. The boy's first of such prizes. He'd been promptly swindled of one of the guns in a bet over the height of a sycamore fated for firewood. That left him one pistol and five balls for the smoothbore barrel. Two went to target practice, one to drunken roistering, one to a duel with a blue jay on a fencepost (lost), and the last plumb lost along the way.

He could only wait now for another of his comrades to fall. Be first to scavenge.

"Hey, Swinney," he called. "You think they're down there?"

"Somebody is," said the fat man, turning back down the line.

The boy sat his horse and made ready to maraud. When their leader rode past, the boy could smell him. The Colonel was riding the line with words of exhortation, of glory and honor and duty and triumph. Then he rode out into the light and struck his saber heavenward, no gleam upon the corroded blade. They spurred their horses' bellies at the slashed order of charge and dropped down into the valley upon a thunder of hooves.

The cavalcade fanned out as they descended, tearing divots from the soft turf. The boy, so scant of weight, pulled ahead of many in the onrush. He was not first to the house but first onto the porch, his horse needing no dally to stay her should shots be fired. The porch planks gave beneath his boots, sodden or thin-cut or both. The door was standing wide and he ducked into the sudden dark. Pistol first, knife second. The ceilings were low, the furniture neat. No roaches scattered before him. No people. Other men clamored through the door behind him. Outside, war whoops and the squealed slaughter of pig.

No one in the front rooms, the rear, the kitchen. He found the stairs and shot upward into the blue dark of the second floor, the balls of his feet hardly touching the steps, the drop-point of his blade plumbing the gloom ahead like a blind man's stick. The curtains were all drawn, the floor dark. He stepped from one room into another. Quilted beds neatly made, wardrobe of cheap wood. Then he crossed the threshold into still another room, this the darkest.

He swung the pistol toward her white back, the dark hair all upon its contours like a black eddy of streamwater. She had not heard him, was watching the other door. Her thin shift was open at the back, skin pale as bone. He swallowed, suddenly nervous, and realized how hungry he was, his stomach drawn up empty inside him. Heart, heart, heart again. It sounded in the cavity of his chest. The pistol began to quiver like a pistol should, whelmed with power.

His voice a whisper: "Ma'am?"

She spun on bare feet, kitchen knife clutched to chest, face silly-hard with courage, fear.

"Which side?" she asked him.

"It don't matter which."

She was not looking at him, not listening either, staring instead into the black tunnel of the barrel like she might jam the pike by willpower alone.

He looked at her and then at the gun, kinking his wrist to better see the thing. An object foreign to him. He lowered it to his side and sheathed the knife as well and the two of them stood staring at one another, unspeaking.

"What's your name?" he asked finally, dry-mouthed, his words hardly crossing the six feet of space that separated them.

She pointed the kitchen knife at him.

"Nancy. Any closer and I kill you."

The floorboards jolted, steps upon the stairs. He shot across to her, past the blade.

"You got to hide."

"Nowhere to," she said. "I'll take my chances."

"They ain't good."

A bearded sharecropper with tobacco-juiced lips, black-gritted, clopped into the room. A Walker Colt hung loosely in his hand. He saw the girl and smiled.

"Christmas early," he said.

The boy stood beside the girl, mouth agape. She spoke to him without looking.

"You a man or I got to protect my own self?"

His mouth closed. Slowly he raised the dueling pistol ornate and empty at the older man's heart.

"I don't reckon it's Christmas yet," he said.

The man spat a black knot on the floor and leveled his Colt at the boy, casual-like.

"Now, Mr. Walker here, he beg to differ."

The boy went to thumb the hammer back but back it was.

"Where them pistol tricks, boy?"

"Don't reckon I need them."

Black caulking divided the man's teeth.

"You killed yet?"

"Plenty."

"No. I knowed you was a virgin the day we took you on. I knowed by plain sight and I know it still. You want to be a man? Tell you what, I'll let you watch."

The fingers of his free hand began to unbutton his britches and he began to walk slowly across the room, legs straddled.

The boy put the palm of his hand against the girl's belly to push her behind him and her waist was as tiny and delicate as his idea of what was fragile in the world. When he touched her she touched him back, her hand warm on his.

"No," said the boy to the sharecropper. "No."

The man kept coming.

"No."

At the last the boy lunged unsheathing his knife and a

white crack exploded inside his head and dreaming or dying he felt his blade plunge into the liquid underbelly of all that could have happened. All that would have. He saw her eyes come over him, blue-rimmed, the pupils deep and black and wide as wells. All for him. Then darkness.

Hands upon his face, his brow. Palms smooth. Tough but smooth, callous-shaven. No scratching, no frictive grit. A voice like running water. The layers that bound him were cut away, piece by piece, until he was naked, unwooled, committed to dark.

More voices over him, whispers and orders he could not decipher. Instead he drifted in a world his own, dark with nightmare. Infection. Dreams of his past, fevered, like his first landing on this shore. The men he pushed under, the men that pushed him. Ladders of them, limb-conjoined, wanting for air. The spouts of exhalation, gargle-mouthed. The groan of the ship sinking beneath them, sucking them under. The white jet of expelled air, last of the pockets that saved him. That shot him to the surface, white-birthed.

Then and now black-whirled. Nightmare and memory.

The ship gone, the waves high. The pale slit of coast, like snow. The beach underneath his feet, a new land. The mad stumbling in darkness, black mobs of fliers enraptured by his flesh. Then the lop-sided shack, the man called Swinney who fed him pork and whiskey, who took him in, and then the Colonel, who took them all. After that the foreign land grown mountainous, and meaner, and scarecrow men who haunted ridges, and rib-boned horses beneath them, and always the hunger, insatiable, and the wagons raided, and the barns and the farmhouses, and never so much blood.

With these fever-dreams came the vomiting. Hours or days long. Hot on his chest, aprons of himself expelled. Sickness and sweat and instruments on his skin, metal-cold.

One day he could hear the words of the men over his sickbed:

"How long's he been like this?"

"Near a week. Took that long to find you."

"How old is he?"

"Couldn't really say, Doc."

"He's hardly even whiskered."

"Well."

"Well, where did he come from?"

"Shipwreck off the coast, blockade-runner."

"Immigrant? Another Irish, with sympathies?"

"Don't talk like it. Talks like you or me."

"Not anymore he won't. Not if this fever don't break."

"You best hope he do, Doc."

"Shall I, Mr. Swinney?"

"Otherwise you might find yourself there beside him. Untongued."

"Where is your commanding officer?"

"Don't you worry your head about it."

"Where is he?"

"With the girl. And you, Doc. You with me."

Minutes or hours or days later the sickbed gone, the house too, his world beginning to sway and totter beneath him, uncertain of step. It expanded and collapsed and sweated and snorted, a ribbed joinery articulating beneath him as though the surface of the world sprung from engines hot and deep beneath the soil and rock.

Sometimes he could not sit the horse, too weak, so they laid him belly-down across the torso of a horse with no saddle, his head lying against one of the flaring sides. In daylight the sun leered sickeningly above him, the trees all warped and gnarled, the world ugly and pale and mean. He shut his eyes against the light. Nightfall he was led stumbling to void himself in the trees, liquid and quaking.

A round man, gone strange to him, leading him, an animal on a rope.

His strength returned slowly, his lucidity too. One day he awoke on the back of the horse. The light was slanted, late afternoon, and he was mad with hunger. He tried to wrestle loose and found himself rope-bound to the animal like a sack of feed or beans or other provision.

The troop stopped just before nightfall. He called out when someone walked past, his voice strange with disuse. Before long another man stood beside him, unhitching the ropes with thick fingers. He slid to the ground and leaned against the horse. The blood receded slowly from his vision leaving old Swinney standing there before him, loose loops of rope in his hand. The boy rubbed the furrows of chafed skin at his wrists. He touched his head lightly, the bandage, the long crust of blood.

"I a prisoner, Swinney?"

Swinney shook his head.

"No, boy."

"Should I be?"

"Colonel said you done him a favor puncturing that son of a bitch."

"So is he—?"

Swinney nodded.

"Bled out. Colonel's orders."

"And the girl?"

Swinney turned from him.

"Come with me, boy. You need to eat."

They walked toward the light of the fire. The boy staggered along behind, finding his legs. He was disoriented, the ground uncertain. He had never been so hungry.

"Where are we?" he asked Swinney.

"Few days north of that farmhouse. You was sick for near on two weeks."

The boy nodded. "North," he said, low.

Swinney looked at him a long moment. His belly shook. "Lucky dog," he said. He turned.

The boy thought to say something, but nothing came.

He followed the old man the rest of the way to the fire, man and horse glazed with flame. The boy sat on the white heart of a hickory stump, and the others showed him their smiles, yellow-toothed, dark-gummed. They handed him a tin of stewed pork and he slurped down its contents in a single go.

When he handed back the empty tin he saw the sleeve of his coat.

One of the men leaned into the fire, showing his face.

"She sewn it for you," he said.

"We had to cut away your old," said Swinney. "We was going to give you Oldham's."

"Oldham?" said the boy.

"Man you killed," said somebody. "Probably you ought to know his name."

"You know all their names?" the boy asked him.

A chuckle rose multi-lunged from men's chests, choral.

"She wasn't wanting you to wear Oldham's," said Swinney. "She sewn you that one out of old what-have-you."

"Rags and quilts and such."

"Bedsheets too."

"I heard scraps of old Oldham hisself."

"A coat of many colors."

"Yea," said another man. "Like Joseph's of old."

The boy held the sleeves toward the fire's orbit. Ribbons and patches of cloth cross-laced the coat, thick-stitched. He stood among the men and worked his arms inside the coat and found the cut of it closer than any he'd ever worn, his small frame normally swallowed in volumes of wool. This one hugged him like a second skin. He thought of who stitched it, of how she must know the contours that shaped him.

"How is she?" he asked them.

They rustled. No one spoke.

"What the hell y'all done to her?"

The boy looked around, his face darkened.

"Should I of stuck every last one of you? That it?"

One man, then another, put a hand to his knife.

Swinney stepped forward. He cleared his throat.

"We left her," he said. "She ain't none of your concern."

"Says who?"

"Says the Colonel."

The boy looked to where the Colonel's fire flickered a good ways off. He knew he should lower his voice, but didn't.

"What does he care?"

Swinney let his hands fall open, silent.

The boy looked at him, his eyes slowly widening.

"The Colonel is married," he said.

The men shifted on their blankets and stumps. The boy looked at them a long moment.

His voice was low: "He's had his way, then."

They said nothing. Their assent.

He whispered it, the question that remained: "Against her will?"

None of the men looked at him. They looked at the fire or their hands or their boots but not at him. The boy swallowed thickly and thumbed the bandage on his head.

"So be it," he said. He sat back on the stump and stared into the fire.

Sometime later he spoke up:

"Say, I get something outta all this?"

Swinney pulled something from his coat and the men handed it one to the next circling the firelight until the woolen sock, heavy as a giant's foot, arrived in the boy's hand. He slipped off the sock and the Walker Colt sat in his lap, the crescent pearl of the grip like a tiny moon.

"You earned it," said Swinney.

"Yeah you did," said somebody else.

The boy pointed the pistol into the dark of the man's voice.

"Five shots left," he said. "One in my head."

Nobody spoke, and he knew they wondered what spirits might have snuck through that wound of his. Into his skull. What demons. He did not feel like a boy anymore. He felt old as any of them. Older.

He rode for three days among them, quiet. Alien. Waiting.

One night Swinney pulled him aside.

"What the hell is wrong with you?" he asked.

"Tell me how to get back."

"You got to be shitting me."

"Tell me," said the boy.

The third night he lay down to rest early. The cold was coming down out of the north and the ground could keep a man from sleeping if he didn't get to sleep early enough, with some sunlight still left in the dirt, the rock.

After a time the boy rose from his pallet of old sacks amid the snoring of his compatriots and moved toward the far off embers of the Colonel's fire, silent as a wraith, one hand on the grip of his pistol to mask its glow.

When he passed Swinney he saw two white orbs look at him. Just as quick they disappeared, closed, and whatever they saw prompted no movement.

The boy kept on picking his way among the stones, the heads, and making no shadow, no sound. The coals of the Colonel's fire glowed red, the flames low. His black stallion stood fifteen hands tall, thick-muscled, big haunches twitching in his sleep. Unsaddled. The boy did not see the saddle but he saw the Colonel's slouch hat lying there beside him, the twin tassels still gold even for all they'd rode above.

The boy pulled back the sleeve of his new coat and crouched, slow to lessen the crackling of his boots, and took the hat by the hand indentions over the crown. As he turned to the horse the shadow of the round brim crossed the Colonel's face like a black halo. The boy saw him shift, his hand groping the butt of the pistol under his bedroll.

By the time the Colonel sat upright he found himself all alone, his gun pointed toward empty space. Leaves, firespangled, quivering where the horse had been, hoof prints welled with firelight.

The boy laid his cheek low against the horse's neck as they crashed through underbrush and low-hanging limbs. He hit upon an old wagon road whose dust shone white and crooked down the mountain switchbacks. The company shunned such roads where spies could estimate the size of their force, where they could be detected at all. They took horse trails or even game trails instead, or they cut their own where the brush grew thick. The boy had the strongest horse underneath him and he was the lightest rider to boot and he believed he might outrun on the open road whomever they sent to catch him.

He dropped down, down out of the mountains in darkness. His breath and the breath of the horse and the dust of the road all mingling into a white plume that rode upon their heels like some hounding ghost of their own making. He thought of the men pursuing them, men with feathers of dead birds in their hats and guns of many hands come to rest finally in their black-creased palms.

First light rose colorless over the hills crumpled and creased into one another like a sheet enameled over a miscellany of untold items, of corpses and rock and whatever else gave the earth its shape. Sparse trees bristled from the hillsides gold-leafed, a touch of red. The season was turning, so fast. He had been out of the world for what seemed an eternity and if he could just see her he thought she might embrace him surely as the coat she'd made him. Their courtship so short, seconds alone, but the true shape of him displayed forevermore in the event that split them. He thought this would count above all else.

At a high outcropping of rock he dallied the horse and climbed to the flattop to surveil the terrain behind him, the terrain ahead. Dust rose from the road far behind him. Whether of riders in pursuit he could not say. Plenty others traveled these roads. Couriers, runaways, men of uniformed war. Militia and home guard too. Enemies all for a boy of his position and exploits.

He let the horse drink at a rock-strewn stream and drank some himself and set off again. In daylight he left the main road and traveled parallel, rounding into and out of sight of its commerce, his path much slowed over the closed ground. When darkness fell he returned to the road and the gallop.

Day and night he rode to see her. His Nancy. Dusk of the third day he rode out onto a ridge and saw farmhouses of the sort he sought. Houses like hers in the valley bottoms. Swaddling them, forests richer with autumn than the forests out of which he rode, more abrupt spurts of red and yellow against the green. Whether by time or altitude he could not say, the land of his home being evergreen, few colors to mark the seasons. His heart swelled upon the vista below him until he saw the black kink of river that lay in his path, no bridge in sight.

He rode down the ridges until he reached the riverbank where the road attenuated into a long white spear under the shallows and disappeared. A wood barge sat beached on the bank, a ferryman dozing on the afterdeck.

The boy hauled the horse to a stop alongside and kicked the hull.

"Hey there."

The ferryman opened one eye beneath the shadow of his cap. He eyed the boy and the horse he rode and the hat he wore.

"Ten bits to cross," he said. "No bartering less you got something to drink."

The boy looked out at the flat river, the black surface vented here and there with hidden currents. Then he looked behind him at the road. Then back again to the river. Deep enough for nightmare.

"Ten bits," said the man again.

"Where's the nearest bridge?" the boy asked him.

"Bridge? Ten bits is cheap, son. Specially for a man with a horse like that one. Course, if you got you a drop of whiskey—"

"I need a bridge, sir. No ferries."

The man looked hurt.

"Well, if you're partial to bridges, the nearest is ten miles yonder. Them partisans blown her last month. Dynamite. But she's still operable, least tolerably. Don't you go telling nobody though. That's in confidence."

He winked.

The boy looked upriver in the direction indicated. Then he tipped his cavalryman's hat at the ferryman.

"I'm much obliged, sir."

As he hauled the horse down to the soft flats of the riverbank, the boy knew his pursuers would learn all they needed to know from this man. They would know what condition he was in, what condition his horse. They would know what direction he was headed, how much ground they could gain on him by taking the ferry. And, most of all, they would know he was not a boy without fear.

He stopped the horse a ways down the bank and looked back over his shoulder at the dozing ferryman. The boy knew how he could remove all of that knowledge from the man's head. All that might betray him. And he could prove to them what kind of man he was. A kind better left alone. His fingers touched the butt of the Colt. A long moment later he gripped great fistfuls of the horse's mane and shot away toward the bridge.

He began to catch shapes quivering upon ridges he'd crossed, dust rising from paths he'd taken just hours before. They were gaining. He stopped for nothing. And still they gained.

They overtook him two days later in the valley of the farmhouse. The Colonel and two others. The Colonel riding hatless on a big blood bay and the other two flanking him, the trio breaking from the trees diagonal the boy in a flying wedge, the Colonel leading with his horse-pistol drawn, the others with Spencer repeaters already shouldered like buffalo hunters of the plains.

They headed him off not firing at first to save the horse he rode. They headed him off right before the porch of the house and he called out to her over them and they smiled from behind the long barrels of the weapons with which they would rob him of the chances twice given him at moments of dubious survival. Twice given, twice squandered. This the boy thought as Nancy appeared in the window of the room where he had first and last seen her, where she had perhaps sewn the coat he wore with those white and slender fingers that spread now flatly upon the windowpane like a prisoner's.

"Off the horse," said the Colonel.

He had the bay horse turned broadside the porch steps, the front door.

"Didn't hear you," said the boy, cocking his ear toward him.

A blow landed across his back and he fell forward. His hands streaked across the sweat-slick musculature of the horse, helpless. Too lean to grip. Too hard. He landed shoulder-first in the yard and his breath left him, knocked out of his lungs. He rolled onto his back and looked bleary-eyed at the men and horses, their shapes warped and wavering as those seen from below the surface of a well. He could not get enough air.

The Colonel shucked his near foot from the stirrup and brought his other leg over the pommel and dropped from his horse without ever turning his back. The gaunt hollows of his face, his cheeks, looked down into the boy's. The upturned points of his mustache sat upon his face like a black smile. He reached out of sight and his hand came back placing the slouch hat on his head, pulling the brim into place.

"I give a boy a chance, and look what it gets me. All for a goddamn woman."

"Her name is Nancy," said the boy. "I saved her."

The Colonel pulled him off the ground by the coat.

"But can you save yourself?"

The boy heard the patchwork of colors strain against the stitches that bound them, begin to tear faintly but not to give.

"I saved her," he said.

The butt of the horse-pistol came hard across his temple, his jaw, his nose. Bone and cartilage succumbing to harder matter. The Colonel dropped him brokenly to the ground.

"Get her then," he said. "Go in and get her."

Faintly the boy saw a hand against the sky, a finger pointed heavenward. Wayward from the house, the window. The boy could not see if the Colonel was wearing gloves or if his hand was just that darkened with gunpowder and soot.

"Go get her."

The corners of the boy's vision were closing when he first heard the shots. There were plenty after that, whoops and screams. Ambush. Then silence. Sometime later he found other men around him, strangers, these in uniform. Gray or blue, he could not tell. They asked him who he fought for and what company and what name. Their breath was rancid, their words quick. He could not answer them. They asked him how he came by such a horse and was it not stolen. They asked him whether he was a deserter or a bounty-jumper or a coward or a foreigner and he could not tell them. They told him the men they just killed had died killing him and they could only honor the dead by carrying out their final wishes.

They said they did not want to waste another bullet.

They rode him up onto the ridge where he'd first looked down upon this valley, this state. They slung a rope over a heavy limb and sat him on the horse he'd stolen and slid the noose over his bare neck. There were three of them. He did not fight.

Below him the forests glimmered fire-like in the last rays of sun, colors as brightly variegate as the coat he wore. He could hardly swallow for the snugness of the rope. He looked down at his Nancy, a white cutout in the black upper window, and he was sorry she would remember him this way. He looked down upon that whole country, so pretty in the fall, in the season of blood and gold, and he was no longer a stranger unto the land.

A man now wearing the Colonel's slouch hat stepped forward to bind his hands, another kept a Winchester repeater leveled upon him. The boy put his good hand into his coat. Slowly, to provoke no alarm. They watched him. He pulled the pistol butt-first from where it hung hidden in the folds and offered the pearl grip of it to his captors, one finger on the trigger guard.

"She's a firecracker," he warned, his smile broken in the gathering dusk.

A NOTE FROM THE AUTHOR

There are so many people I would like to thank. My parents, for starters. You guys have always been there, and I'm so grateful, there are no words. I'm not sure God makes better parents. I mean that.

I'd like to thank Kristen. We had some hard times, didn't we? But you always believed, and I won't forget it.

To a big brown wirehaired pointer named Waylon. My buddy. I miss you.

To Heather and Rick for taking a chance on an English major. I'll always be grateful.

Thanks to all my buddies from home and school. You've always been my anchor. You know who you are.

To Dr. Hubert McAlexander, the greatest goddamn English professor who ever lived, or will.

Thanks to all my writing friends here in Wilmington: Lauren and Jason Frye for all the guidance and welcoming me into the "writing group," Majsan Böstrom for all those nights front-porchin' it, and all the guys at the office.

Lastly I'd like to thank Kevin Watson and Christine Norris of Press 53 for welcoming me into the family. I hope to do you proud.

TAYLOR BROWN was born on the Georgia coast. His short fiction has appeared or is forthcoming in *The New Guard*, *The Baltimore Review*, *CutBank*, *The Coachella Review*, *storySouth*, *CrimeSpree Magazine*, the *Press 53 Open Awards Anthology*, and many others. He received the Montana Prize in Fiction for his story "Rider," and he was a finalist for the 2012 Machigonne Fiction Prize. His work has been recognized as one of the "Other Distinguished Mystery Stories" in *Best American Mystery Stories*, and his story "Kingdom Come" won second prize in the 2010 Press 53 Open Awards for Short Story.

He lives in Wilmington, North Carolina, and his website is: www.taylorbrownfiction.com.

Cover artist JORUNN SJOFN lives in Reykjavik, Iceland. She says about her work, "I have a great passion for photography and I love to capture many different things. Since I can remember, I have been interested in taking photos; when I was younger I used to frame everything I saw. I travelled around Iceland a lot with my parents when I was little and loved so many places. Icelandic nature is a big inspiration for me. The light and the unique land-scape is phenomenal and creates endless opportunities. I simply love to capture what I see and share it with the world. I specialize in landscape and nature, but I also take macro pictures and do some artistic work with flowers and other things."

Find more of Jorunn's photography at:
www.flickr.com/photos/jorunns/
www.facebook.com/JorunnSjofnPhotography

CPSIA information can be obtained
at www.ICGtesting.com
Printed in the USA
BVHW031032090819
555497BV00003B/435/P